BLAKE CROUCH
FAMOUS
A NOVEL

Copyright © 2010 by Blake Crouch

Cover art copyright © 2010 by Jeroen ten Berge

All rights reserved.

FAMOUS is a work of fiction. Names, characters, businesses, organizations, places, events, and incidents either are the product of the author's imagination or are used fictitiously. Any resemblance to actual persons, living or dead, events, or locales is entirely coincidental.

For more information about the author, please visit www.blakecrouch.com.

For more information about the artist, please visit www.jeroentenberge.com.

Interior formatting and layout by TERyvisions www.teryvisions.com

ISBN 10: 1460928261
ISBN 13: 978-1460928264

I won't be happy 'til I'm as famous as God.
—**Madonna**

The highest form of vanity is love of fame.
—**George Santayana**

The image is one thing and the human being is another…It's very hard to live up to an image, put it that way.
—**Elvis Presley**

It stirs up envy, fame does.
—**Marilyn Monroe**

He lives in fame that died in virtue's cause.
—**William Shakespeare**

NY

Chapter 1

fame and money ~ James Jansen ~ goes to work ~ gets fired ~ a shopping spree ~ the day of tranquility ~ a $100 haircut ~ the movie premier ~ says goodbye to mom and dad

Let me tell you something about being famous. First off, it doesn't make you depressed or dissociated from humankind. That's all bullshit. Being famous…is like the very best thing in the world. Everybody knows you, everybody loves you, and it's just because you're you. And that's supposed to make you want to eat sleeping pills? Only reason celebrities say fame blows is so we won't hate them. Because if we really knew how happy they are, how incredible it is just to be them, to own the world, we'd hate them, and then they'd just be notorious.

And the money. Jesus. If I hear one more multi-millionaire tell me that money won't make me happy, I'm going to hurt someone. Really.

My name is Lancelot Blue Dunkquist, and the best thing about me is, when you doll me up right, I look like a Movie Star.

I've been mistaken for James Jansen twenty-eight times. Of course you know who James Jansen is. Remember *And Then There Was One?* That's his most successful movie, sorry, film to date. Actors don't make movies. They make films. Anyway, James Jansen played the detective. You know the part at the end where the guy walks in on the bank robbery and he's only got one bullet left? He knows he's dead, but he stares down the two robbers and says, "By God you may walk out of here with that money, but which one of you is it going to be?" What a line.

I'm actually an inch taller than James Jansen, but you see, this works to my advantage, because when people see me, they're thinking *It's JJ! He's larger than life!*

Yes. I am larger than life.

In my real life, I work as a legal secretary in a patent firm in Charlotte, North Carolina. It's very convenient, because I live just up the interstate in Huntersville, above the garage in my parents' house. A perfect setup really. I get to use Mom's car four days a week (on Tuesdays she takes me to work and picks me up, because she volunteers in the office of their Baptist church). Dad doesn't even make me pay rent, so I'm saving money like crazy. As of my last bank statement, $41,617.21 was simmering in my money market account.

I usually wake up at 6:45 a.m. Lewis Barker Thompson Hardy is quite the casual work environment. Since the thirty-five attorneys only practice corporate patent law, we rarely have clients in the office. So the dress code is extremely lax. Today for instance, I'm sporting gray sweatpants, a T-shirt, and Adidas flip-flops.

I'm running later this morning, but normally I arrive at our building around 8:10. I always park in a visitor space since they're the closest to the main entrance.

Our offices are located on the seventh floor, but I only take the elevator if I have it all to myself. I don't excel at chitchatting with people. I learned this neat trick: once I'm inside, I press seven, and then as long as I hold the button down, the elevator won't stop until it reaches our floor. But I don't even like riding by myself. The walls consist of mirrors, and the light is dim and eerie.

So nine times out of ten, I huff it up the stairwell like I'm doing today, downside being that I'm always sweaty when I reach our floor.

Our suite is already in full operation when I enter. Heading through the conference room into the break room, I open one of the four refrigerators and stow the lunch mom prepared for me inside.

I walk down the hallway. File Rooms A-D are on the right, the partners' offices on the left. Through their windows, I see morning light spreading over the green piedmont forest and reflecting off a distant pond. I always see that glinting pond on the way to my desk, except when it's cloudy. The buildings of uptown Charlotte shimmer in early sun.

At the end of the hall, I enter the large room of cubicles. Mine sits in the center grouping. It's very neat. The other paralegals keep messy workstations. They're more concerned with plastering the walls with pictures of their husbands and children. I don't display any pictures. The only non-work-related item I have is a cutout from a magazine article in *Hollywood Happening*. I taped it to the top of my monitor a year ago. It's just two letters: JJ. Janine once asked me what it meant, but I didn't tell her.

I turn on my computer and pull out a case file I've been working on since Friday. My duties involve corresponding with clients. It's not terribly exciting stuff… Dear Mr. Smith: We are pleased to inform you that the above-identified U.S. patent application has been granted a Notice of Allowance by the United States Patent and Trademark Office…that sort of thing.

I'm getting ready to begin the first letter of the day when footsteps stop at my cubicle.

"Lance?"

I swivel around. It's Janine, the Office Manager. The other paralegals despise her. I don't really have an opinion. She's kind of pretty—highly blond, tan, quite a dresser.

"Jeff wants to see you in his office first thing."

"Now?"

"First thing."

I follow Janine back up the hallway, watching the points of her high heels leave tiny, diminishing marks in the avocado carpet.

Jeff has a corner office. He's the Hardy from Lewis Barker Thompson Hardy. I wonder why she's leading me to his office, as if I don't know where it is.

Partner Jeff is dictating a patent application when Janine pokes her head through the doorway.

"Jeff, Lance is here to see you," she says reverently. He's the scary partner.

He stops the recorder, says, "Send him in and shut the door."

I walk inside and sit down in a chair in front of his desk. The door closes behind me. Jeff is thin-lipped and very sleek, and the only time he smiles is when he speaks to one of the other partners.

He just stares at me. I look out the windows. I count the framed diplomas and plaques on his walls (nineteen). His desk is buried under case files. There's a stack of resumes and cover letters on the floor by my feet. I've just begun to read the body of the top letter when Jeff says, "Lance, how long have you been here?"

"Five years next month."

I try to meet his eyes. I can't. He's so intelligent—only 34 or 35. I'm 38. I could be his big brother. I tell myself this over and over but it doesn't help. I stare out the window again at the Charlotte skyline. I wish I could see the pond from his office. I feel the zeroing-in of his glare, smell waves of his cologne lapping at my face. His suit looks so expensive. Custom-tailored even.

"Lance, you heard of eye contact?"

I meet his eyes.

"Why are you sweating, Lance?"

"I, uh, took the stairs up."

Opening a drawer, he pulls out a 9" by 12" Tyvex envelope and tosses it into my lap. Our return address label has been circled and "Return To Sender" stamped on the envelope. "We received that in the mailroom Friday afternoon. Take out the letter."

I remove the single sheet of paper.

"Recognize that, Lance?"

"No."

"You should. You wrote it for me a week ago. See your initials at the bottom?" Beneath Jeff's signature, I see JH:lbd. I'm lbd.

"I remember this now," I say.

"Look at the envelope."

I look at the envelope.

"You sent it to the wrong client." He pauses to let the weight of this crush me. "Dr. David Dupree, to whom you misdirected it, fired us this morning, before you graced us. He called me and said, among other things: 'if you aren't taking care of your other clients, how do I know you're taking care of me?' He's got a point."

"I'm sorry. That was just—"

"A big fuck-up, Lance. A big fucking fuck-up. Do you know what we invoiced him for last month?" I shake my head. "$8,450.00 *I* invoiced him for that. And that was a light month. I was on the verge of writing five new patent applications for him. You cost this firm money. You cost me money. Go clear out your cube."

I stand. My head throbbing. Jeff stands, too, his eyes wide and angry. I look out the windows, Charlotte Douglas International Airport visible in the distance, the speck of a jet lifting off a runway.

"Here's a tip," he says. "When you go in for your next job interview, dress like you give a shit. No one appreciates you walking around here like a slob. This isn't your living room. It's my office. It's the office of hard-working, brilliant men."

My face is hot. I can stare at him now.

"Don't talk to me like I'm nothing. I could be your big brother."

"Get out of my office."

The first thing I do is drive to the bank since it's just down the street from the building where I used to work. I walk in and tell the teller to transfer everything from my money market to my checking account. Then I withdraw $2,000 in cash, slip her a twenty for her trouble, and drive uptown.

It doesn't really hit me that I've been fired until I'm walking in the cool, spring shadow of the First Union Tower. I'd planned to work until I saved up $50,000, but I think I can manage on what I have. It feels surprisingly good to be unemployed, especially at this early hour of a Monday morning, when thousands of people are just beginning their workday all around me.

The store I'm looking for is on the corner up ahead—McIntyre's Fine Men's Clothing. I've heard their advertisements on the radio.

Inside, an exquisitely-dressed older gentleman puts down a sweater he's folding and comes over.

"My name is Bernard. May I help you find something?"

"I want the most expensive suit in the store."

"Well, why don't you follow me." He leads me over to the dressing rooms. "Have a seat. I'll be right back."

I sit down, the only customer in the store. The smell of clean, unworn fabric engulfs me.

Bernard returns carrying a jacket in each hand. One is dark blue, one dark gray.

"I'm sorry, I didn't get your name."

"Lance."

"Well, Lance, I'm holding the two finest suits in the store. You're a forty-two, right?"

"I don't know."

"You're a 42. At any rate, they're both Hugo Boss. One hundred percent wool. Single breasted. Three buttons. Very smart."

James Jansen wore a gray suit in the movie *The Defendant*. He played a man wrongly accused of murder. It almost won him an Oscar.

"The gray one."

"Well, why don't we try it on then?" Bernard opens one of the dressing rooms and hangs up the gray one. "Let me just measure your neck and we'll get you a crisp Oxford shirt to go with it."

I lay my gray Hugo Boss across the backseat of Mom's Buick, drop the four bags containing slacks, socks, three pairs of shoes, belts, silk mock-turtlenecks, polo shirts, and Oxfords in the trunk, and set out for Salon 87, several blocks up the street.

The chic receptionist informs me that I'm lucky. They're normally much too busy for walk-ins. She gives me a brochure to choose which treatment package is right for me, but I don't have time to read the thing. Celebrities are always pressed for time.

"Just give me the most expensive package you offer," I tell her. "Money is no object."

"Fantastic, then I'll put you down for the Day of Tranquility."

The next six hours are almost unbearable, but I have to cleanse myself of Lancelot, so I let the "pampering specialist" have free reign over my entire body, even my feet which are fairly hideous.

I get a facial, body exfoliation, clay treatment, a massage, seaweed body wrap, 15 minutes of reflexology, and finally, a shampooing and hair-styling.

The stylist, Roger, asks before he starts if I have a particular look in mind.

"James Jansen."

"Sure. You know…oh my God, you could be his twin!"

I just smile.

I think Roger is gay. At least I hope. If I'm paying a hundred dollars for a haircut, the stylist damn well better be a homosexual, because from what I hear, they can really cut some hair.

My flight will depart Charlotte at 8:20 tomorrow morning, so when I arrive home a little before five, I head directly up to my room with the day's purchases and drag my single piece of luggage out from under the bed.

My room is not, as you probably fear, a tribute to James Jansen. I don't have a closet full of candles and pictures and articles of his clothing. No posters of him on my walls. I don't even own all twenty-four of his movies. See, this is the thing—I don't love him. I'm sure he has fans more rabid than me. I'm only intrigued by him because we share a close resemblance. The obsession stems from the opportunities this affords me, not the man himself.

Mom has cooked shepherd's pie for supper again. The three of us always eat together in the den and watch *Entertainment Magazine*. I'm not going to miss sitting on the sofa between them with our trays.

Entertainment Magazine is particularly interesting tonight. The show is broadcasting live from a movie premier. Gives me chills to watch the Stars stroll down the red carpet. So poised. Witty. These are things I have to perfect. I've been practicing. I'm nearly there.

The female host stops one of the Stars of the movie and asks how she's feeling tonight as a thousand fans scream behind her and the SoCal sun falls into the Pacific.

"Well, you know, I love this part of it. The work's done. And you know, John was just so great to work with. I was a little intimidated before I met him, because, he's John, you know? But he really treated me like an equal, a colleague, and as a result, I think we've made a fabulous film."

Beautiful. See how she complimented her costar while at the same time bringing glory to herself? That's a professional.

After dinner, Dad turns off the television. We're all sitting there with our trays in the silence of the living room. There's a painting of Jesus above the TV set that's been on that wall since I was a kid. Kind of a strange place to put the Lord. I don't know.

In a minute, Dad will get up and go to bed since he's boozed out of his mind on Aristocrat gin. Mom will go clean up the kitchen and read her Bible. I'll retire to my room above the garage, and while I pack, watch a Jansen movie and several episodes of *Hollywood Starz!* (I tape them. They're fascinating studies in Star behavior).

"I have something to tell you guys," I say. "I'm leaving for New York tomorrow morning."

"What for?" Mom asks.

I put my arms around the both of them. Not because I really want to. Just seems like the thing to do.

"Since I dropped out of college nineteen years ago, this has been my home. But I've had a dream, Mom, Dad. And dreams cost money. I've saved my money for this dream, and now the time has come for me to go after it."

They don't know what the devil I'm talking about. I haven't told anyone my plans.

Mom begins to tear up.

Dad doesn't say anything. He kind of nods. Then he gets up, pats me on the shoulder, and walks out of the room. He doesn't mean anything by it. He's just genuinely not interested in much these days.

Mom and I sit on the couch for awhile. I look around the living room seeing as how this will be the last time I see it for awhile. Maybe ever. Such a normal-looking house. Smells like cabbage. Always has.

Mom's bottom lip quivers. She rests her head against my shoulder. I'm not convinced she's really sad. Sure she'll miss me, but I think they've been hoping this day would come for quite awhile.

Chapter 2

*through the portal ~ first class ~ Miss Lavender Suit
~ The Way ~ 29*

With a boarding pass in hand and my luggage checked, I stroll toward the metal detector, imagining it's a portal, and that once I cross the threshold, I cease to be Lancelot Blue Dunkquist.

My pace quickens. I walk straight, confident, and tall through the terminal, relishing that transient airport smell but maintaining the stoic façade the great Stars don in public.

I am James Jansen.

I am James Jansen.

James Jansen is flying out of Charlotte, North Carolina this morning. James Jansen sports a gray Hugo Boss with a T-shirt underneath (Stars can get away with it), and shoes as mirror-black as volcanic glass. He is clean-shaven, his hair an immaculate brown mane of style. He is larger than life. Oblivious to the mundane act of walking through an airport. This concourse is only a channel transporting him from one place where he is the focus, to another. He is bigger than all of this. He is electric.

I take my seat in first class by the window. Before the coach crowd starts to file in, a flight attendant stops to ask what I'd like to drink. Bottled water. She looks at me kind of funny, half-smirking like she suspects I'm somebody she's seen before. Makes my stomach flutter. But she doesn't ask. I'm sure *first-class* flight attendants see the Stars on a regular basis. They're probably told not to bother them.

I don't look at the coachers as they trudging past me toward the back of the plane. I stare contemplatively out the small window at the distant pines which frame the tarmac. But I can feel people staring at me as they pass, and man it feels good.

So the jet's loaded up and I think we're getting ready to taxi on out of here when a woman in a lavender business suit steps into the cabin. Her hair is mussed, as they say, like she just sprinted through the airport. Wouldn't you know it—she sits next to me, and I start to get all flushed like I normally do when interaction with people is imminent.

Our eyes meet, and what I do next is what clinches it. I cut this smile I've been practicing for ten years. Jansen possesses an unmistakable grin: he smiles quick, and only from the right corner of his mouth like he's had a stroke or something. But it works. It's playful, mischievous, and I've got it down cold. In fact, when I flash it, I actually see it take her breath away. The realization of who I am spreading blatantly across her face, glossy lips parting, but she doesn't say anything. She catches herself, smiles back, and turns her attention to the fastening of her seatbelt.

As we go airborne and I feel that funny pressure against my chest, I wonder if Partner Jeff is looking out the window of his magnificent office. I think I'd like for him to see me in this moment. He'd probably respect what I'm doing. Ambitious people admire the hell out of other ambitious people. We're all in this big secret club.

After I get bored of looking out the window, I glance at the woman beside me. Her briefcase is open on her lap and she's sorting through some papers. Bet she's too shy to initiate a conversation, but unfortunately, I can't do it. See, Stars *never* initiate conversations with non-Stars. It's one of the most important rules. I probably shouldn't even realize that another human being is even sitting beside me, because I'm so engrossed in myself.

So here's what I do.

Since Miss Lavender Suit is so focused on her briefcase, I reach down and lift my leather satchel from under the seat. Then I unbuckle the strap, throw back the flap, and pull out a script. There's this website you can go to that has all the scripts from practically every movie ever made. Few weeks ago, I ordered one for this movie made fifteen years back that nobody ever saw. I hadn't even heard of it.

The movie was called "The Way," about this married guy who gets dissatisfied with his life and winds up going to the Amazon Jungle or someplace like that. They didn't even have it on Netflix, so I had to buy a used copy on eBay. I can see why it wasn't very popular. It's almost four hours, and the only good part comes near the end where the guy goes native with this tribe. At least if going native means what I think it means. I never looked it up or anything.

So I pull out this script, and then I lower my tray and set my bottled water and glass of ice down so I can pretend to read the thing. Man, does Miss Lavender Suit get interested in a hurry. I mean, if I hadn't been watching to see if she was interested, I probably wouldn't have noticed. But I have my radar out, and she's cutting peeks left and right. I figure she'll be initiating a conversation any minute now, but she keeps clammed up like you wouldn't believe.

Once we hit cruising altitude, I have to pee. I start to take the script with me, since I'm a Star and all and not supposed to trust anybody, but I don't want her to think I'm reading on the toilet. Besides, I'll bet the balance of my checking account that while I'm gone she steals a nice long glance at that script. So I just close the booklet and leave it face-up in my seat.

She doesn't have to stand up to let me out, first class being roomier than coach. Instead, she does that thing where she moves her legs to the side, so I can slide by. Man, I love that. We also meet eyes again, and she's looking at me like I've never been looked at before.

While I'm in the microbathroom, I think of what I'll do if she doesn't say anything. But I don't stay in there long, because Stars don't do disgusting, ordinary things like taking a shit.

When I come back out, she does that thing with her legs again while I ease back into my seat. I lift the script and open it again. Then I give her one more opportunity. I thumb through a few more pages, let out this big sigh, and drop it back into my satchel like I've had it or something. Not real serious. Just annoyed.

And then she does it, and my heart nearly comes up my throat.

"Excuse me," she says, "I swear I'm not one of those people who freaks out when they see somebody famous, but you're James Jansen, aren't you?"

"I am."

"I just wanted to tell you how much I admire your films. You're one of my favorite actors."

"That's very kind of you to say."

Man, my heart is racing, but I manage to hold myself together, because this happens to me all the time. Nothing new about it.

"I'm Denise." She offers her hand, which I accept. It's a bit sweaty. I'm making her sweat.

"Jim."

"Are you uh…oh forget it. I don't want to bother you."

"It's fine. You aren't bothering me, Denise."

"Are you reading a script for a potential movie? If you're allowed to talk about it, I mean."

"I am. Friend of mine who happens to be a director slipped me this script a few months ago. I hadn't had a chance to read it until now. Between you and me, I don't think I'm going to do it."

"Are you working on anything right now?" she asks.

The real Jansen is not. He hasn't done a movie in three years. I have to keep tabs on that sort of thing unless I run into a real Jansen fanatic.

"Not at the moment," I say. "But I am looking at doing some theatre."

"Is that why you're going to New York?"

"Exactly."

"What play are you considering?"

"I really shouldn't say anything yet, since I haven't met with the director."

"Oh, of course, I'm sorry."

I glance out the window, just to make sure we aren't plummeting earthward. To be honest, flying sort of scares me. I've only flown once before.

Below, the land is very rumpled and green—the Appalachians.

"What do you do, Diane?" I ask, intentionally forgetting her name to see if she lets it slip.

"I'm a consultant for brokerage firms," she says, nodding like it's such a commonplace job and she's a little embarrassed to tell me. "I've got several meetings over the next week in New York. Can I ask you something?" she says, leaning in.

"Sure."

"I read once somewhere that you remember every line from every film you've ever done. Is that true?" It is true. Jansen is smart as hell.

I say, "Well, I do have a photogenic memory."

For some reason, Denise laughs and takes a magazine from her briefcase. I'd like to know where she's staying in New York. The real Jansen isn't married. I almost ask her if she'd care to have a drink one evening in the city, but before I do, I try to see her through Jansen's eyes. Through eyes that can have any woman they want. Don't get me wrong. Denise is a very attractive woman, but Jansen grazes in the stratosphere. She's the-most-beautiful-woman-on-the-plane attractive, not Hollywood attractive, so I don't ask. Nothing against her. If I were me, I'd ask her out without a thought. She's as far beyond Lancelot as Jansen is beyond her.

Chapter 3

the worst hotel in the world ~ what it smells like ~ Columbia ~ Professor Wittig ~ funnel cakes on 5th Ave. ~ O. Wilde's ~ vodka, one ice cube, no lime

I'll be honest with you—I don't know the first damn thing about New York. I grew up in the South, and I only visited the city once with my parents when I was thirteen, and that was only for a night.

But I do know one thing going in. It's expensive as hell. Which is why I don't bother to reserve a room at some swanky hotel near Times Square. Instead, I tell the taxi driver at La Guardia that I'm going to a hotel on 227th Street. That's Edenwald. The Bronx. And I know a lot of bad shit goes down there, as they say, but I really don't care. In a way, if I got knifed or something, it wouldn't bother me at all. I'm not saying I'm looking to get knifed. It just wouldn't be the end of the world.

So I check into this perfectly terrifying hotel, and I'll bet every hooker in New York has been in my room, because the place smells like a blowjob. But hey, for $100 a night, I'm not complaining. And I check in for a whole week. I'll bet no one in the history of this place has ever stayed longer than thirty minutes.

I unpack my things. My window overlooks some public housing project, and I sit on the sill for awhile and watch these kids throwing dice for money on the steps of an apartment building.

It makes me nervous as hell leaving my belongings here, but it's only one o'clock. I've got the whole afternoon ahead of me.

So I step out into the hall and lock the door. The carpet is squishy. Someone grunts in a nearby room.

I take the stairs down four dusty flights, and then I'm standing on the sidewalk. Man, is it hot for mid-May. I never noticed the smell of a real city before—oily concrete and concentrated exhaust, like the greasy innards of a car engine. And it's noisy. Not loud noisy. Busy noisy. Like a hundred thousand little sounds all coming together to make one city sound.

A cab finally shows the hell up and I tell the Somali fellow to take me to Columbia University.

My heart starts going as I walk into Dodge Hall, home to Columbia's School of the Arts.

First door on my left is closed, but I can hear someone speaking inside.

"It's the idea of dirty pantyhose, Dan. You're sick."

Another voice: "Lauren, you rushed that last bit."

I continue on, the walls papered with audition notices and advertisements for upcoming productions.

I'm still wearing my sunglasses, because that's another rule. The bigger the Star, the darker the environment in which they're allowed to wear shades, even dim corridors like this one where I can hardly see the first damn thing.

I knock on the door of Professor Paul Wittig's office.

Maybe I'll tell you how I found out about him later. I'm an excellent researcher.

This small, very Jewish man opens the door and looks up at me through glasses without lenses.

I remove my deep dark shades.

"May I help you?" he says. He has thinning gray hair, a charcoal beard.

"Professor Wittig?"

"Yes?"

He looks highly intelligent. That's probably why he doesn't recognize me yet—he's been in his office thinking so hard.

"I was looking for Jerry Boomhower. He has an office down the hall, but he isn't in. I wanted to drop in, surprise him."

"Jerry's taking the summer off."

"Oh, okay. Yeah. Hmm. Well, I was just in the city, wanted to see him. Thanks." Wittig nods curtly and starts to shut his door, but I stop him. "Say, I'm here for a couple days, and I was hoping to see some first-rate theatre. Not Broadway bullshit. Something cutting edge."

Wittig really looks at me for the first time.

"Oh, I'm sorry." I extend my hand. "Jim Jansen."

"Paul Wittig," he mumbles, and man does his interest level rise. His eyes get very twinkly. "What an honor. My goodness. You have no idea how much I admire your work."

"Oh, thank you. That's very kind of you to say."

"I obviously have no manners. Please come in."

I step inside his office and sit down on a leather couch. I figure he's going to take a seat in the matching chair, but instead he sits down beside me and leans back and crosses his legs. He's a superior dresser, one of those guys who look better in slacks and a white linen shirt than most men do in a tux. I can tell he's pretty jazzed to be sitting here with me. He's left his door open, and I'll bet he's praying someone will walk by, catch him shooting the shit with James Jansen. It's understandable. Probably the highlight of his life. That's what being famous is really all about—wherever you go, you're the highlight of everyone's life.

"So are you in town on business, Jim?" he asks, like we're fast friends.

"To be honest, I'm looking at doing some theatre. I've got several months before I start my next project, which incidentally, is about an aspiring actor trying to get work in New York."

"Marvelous, so you're doing a bit of research then."

"Exactly."

"Well, if there's anything I can do to lend some insight, I hope you'll impose on me." He kind of brushes his hand against my knee when he says this, and I'm not sure if it's one of those unconscious brushes or an I-want-to-ride-your-bones brush.

"You know, I may take you up on that," I say, and I sort of graze his knee back with my fingers. Instantly, I regret it, because I can see in his eyes that he's trying to determine whether or not that was a pass.

"Look," he says, "I'm sure you have plans already, but I'm thinking of seeing a show tonight. This off-off thing one of my former students is directing. If you wanted to join me…"

"What's the play called?"

"*Love in the 0's.* It's a one-act. He actually wrote it for his thesis."

"Any good?"

"You've never seen anything like it."

"I did have a dinner party tonight…"

"Don't break your plans."

"No, no, this is a wonderful opportunity. To attend a play with an acting professor. Just the sort of experience I need to really get inside this character I'm going to do. Could you introduce me to the actors afterward? I'd love to get their perspective on the whole theatre scene."

"Absolutely!" He pats my knee again, probably already picturing me at the Academy Awards, Oscar in hand, thanking him in my rambling, charming acceptance speech.

I'm supposed to meet Wittig at this bar on E. 4th Street at 7:30 for pre-show drinks, but there's no way I'm showing up in the same Hugo Boss. When Stars choose to mingle with and be seen by the public, they aren't supposed to wear the same thing for more than several hours. It's a pretty serious rule.

So I catch a cab down to Fifth Avenue and buy this slick Donna Karan and a silk shirt. When I finish shopping, it's nearly three and I realize I haven't eaten anything since my flight this morning. A street vendor is selling funnel cakes sprinkled with powdered sugar. I eat one in the cab on the way back to Edenwald, which takes *forever* to reach.

It's a sizeable relief to walk back into my room. I lock the door and hang my new suit in the tiny closet. It's intolerably hot. I strip down to my underwear and pull a wooden chair over to the window and sit there watching those dice-throwing boys as the afternoon light goes bronze.

O. Wilde's is the first bar I've set foot in since college, and I make sure to show up twenty minutes late, because arriving on time is a sign of pure desperation. It's a loud place across the street from Hamilton Studio, where *Love in the 0's* will be starting in less than an hour.

I spot Wittig standing with his back to the bar, surveying the room. He waves when I enter, wineglass already in hand. I remove my shades and squeeze through the crowd of hipster playgoers, everyone in black like they've all just come from a wake.

Wittig's halfway through a glass of white when I edge up to the bar, and all I can think about is not making an enormous ass of myself when I order Jansen's favorite drink. For people who don't frequent bars, the barkeep is a fairly intimidating persona. They're like oracles or something. See right through you.

"What are you drinking, Jansen?" Wittig asks, real helluva guy-like, and I wonder if he's calling me by my last name so everyone will figure out who he's with.

"I think I'll have my old tried and true," I say as the bartender sidles up.

"Can I get you, sir?"

"Double Absolut with one ice cube. No lime."

"Find the place all right?" Wittig asks while I watch the bartender make my drink.

"Yep."

Wittig's sporting this tweed suit and bowtie that makes him look exceptionally scholarly. Good thing I changed, seeing as how he did.

"Where you staying, Jim?"

"The Waldorf Hysteria. Finally cooling off out there."

"Here you are, sir."

I lift my drink, gaze down at the single cube floating in the vodka.

"That's interesting," Wittig says. "What's with the single piece of ice?"

"One cube cools and dilutes the vodka perfectly." I didn't just make that up. In last January's issue of *Celebrity*, the feature was an interview with Jansen at a bar near his home in the Hollywood Hills. That "one cube cools and dilutes" bit was verbatim what he said to the journalist when asked the same question.

I sip the vodka. Rubbing alcohol. All I can do not to grimace. Jansen's a big drinker. I haven't had a drink since college.

Wittig taps me on the arm, leans over, whispers, "See that table in the corner? Other corner. In about two minutes, those women are going to have the nerve worked up to come over here."

"Yeah, I noticed."

"You want to leave?"

"Paul, if it ever gets to the point where I can't go into a bar and have a drink, I'll quit making movies. Just part of it, you know?"

"No." He smiles. "I don't. Fortunately. Can't imagine what it must be like for you."

I steal another micro-sip of my drink, but it's no use. Oh well. I throw it back in one burning swallow.

"Another, sir?" the bartender asks, before my empty even hits the bar.

"No, I'm good."

Wittig orders another wine.

"So tell me about this play, Paul."

"I think you'll be intrigued. It's Mamet meets Simon meets Pinter meets Beckett. I'm tempted to say more, but I'm afraid it would spoil your experience."

"So am I going to see this kid's stuff on Broadway in the near future?"

"The question, Jim," he points at me, and I hope he isn't getting drunk, "is are you going to see Broadway on Matthew? If he stays true to himself, Broadway will have to come to him. 'Cause I don't see him selling out. This kid is fucking special, Jim."

Everywhere I look, eyes are on me. Male and female. I look at Wittig, his cheeks fire engine red as he knocks back a substantial sip of wine.

"Ready to walk over?" I ask.

I'm ready to get the hell out of O. Wilde's.

I shouldn't be swimming in the deep end my first time in the pool.

Chapter 4

in Hamilton Studio ~ a real piece of shit ~ beholds the city at night ~ offers criticism ~ attends a party ~ strange music ~ meets the director ~ an offer ~ another offer

Lights down. Lights up.

Onstage, a park bench. An overtly fake tree. Cardboard clouds hanging from visible cables.

A man enters stage left, dragging a fake dog by a leash. A woman enters stage right. They stroll starry-eyed toward center stage and bump into each other in front of the bench.

The woman says, "Oh, excuse me. I didn't see you."

"No, no, it's my fault," the man responds. "This damn dog won't heel."

He tugs on the leash, and the stuffed poodle slides across the stage.

"Is your dog stuffed?" she asks.

"Why yes, of course."

"You're walking a fake dog?"

"No, she's real."

The man pulls the dog up into his arms and smothers it with kisses.

"This is Poopsie, yes it is."

Wow.

Thank fucking God it's only one act.

Wittig whispers: "Brilliant opening. You're about to see an entire relationship condensed to thirty minutes. You like it?"

"It's first-rate, Paul."

I have a hard time concentrating on shit, so for the next five minutes I sort of zone out and glance around the theatre. Even though Hamilton Studio is quite small, with only a hundred seats, there's no full house tonight. *Maybe* thirty playgoers. Vivid lighting makes the stage look as sharp as an autumn afternoon.

This woman behind us has a big, sloppy grin across her face, and I wonder if it's because she's enamored with the play, or if she thinks it's comical what gets produced these days.

Now, the man and woman onstage are sitting up in bed.

The man puts a cigarette in his mouth, and the woman removes it.

"Honey, that's so cliché," she says. Then, "You were wonderful."

"I know."

The audience laughs. Not a big laugh. I'd say about a 4 on a scale of 1 to 10.

"How do you know?"

"Because you just told me."

"I mean it," the woman insists. "You really were good."

"I mean it. I know."

More laughter. I gauge it at 8. I even laugh this time, because it is pretty funny. But it doesn't stay funny for long. It gets weird again, and I zone right the hell back out and watch the faces in the audience instead. They're like children, most of them—curious, happy children, trying to see their lives onstage.

Don't ever ask me what *Love in the 0's* was about. Wittig tries explaining it to me in the cab on the way to the director's apartment, says it has to do with the way people like hurting each other. A reaction to the absurd. I don't know. Only reason I care even a little bit is in case I talk to Matthew the director. I mean, I'm not going to tell the guy I didn't know what the hell his play was about.

So I'm sitting in the back, trying to think of something I can say I liked about the thing as the lights of the Village blur by, sidewalks loaded with keen dressers. The city's gorgeous at night. Vital. I roll down my window and the night air rushes hot into my face, perfumed with the smell of garlic and women and spicy meat and coffee beans and storm gutters. For a moment, everything kind of stops, and I'm overwhelmed with this city and this man, Wittig, who I've only known for nine hours, and the fact that I woke up this morning in the room above my parents' garage, and that only yesterday I was fired and had the wherewithal to put this beautiful idea I've been planning for ages into motion. Funny how life goes. The same thing every week, year after year, and then one night you're in a cab in New York City on the way to a party at the apartment of a director whose play you've just seen, and everyone thinks you're a movie Star, and they might just be right.

Wittig pats me on the knee. He's always patting me on the knee.

"You must tell me, Jim. The play—what'd you think?"

"I think your boy Matthew's got a lot on his mind."

"Do tell."

I severely wish he'd just leave it at that, but I can tell he won't.

"I could rave all night," I say. "Let me make one criticism."

"It's our critics who teach us," he says.

I guess you have to say that sort of thing when you're a professor.

"I think Matthew—what's his last name?"

"Gardiner."

"I think Mr. Gardiner is too eager to lecture his audience. There's a certain anxiousness and immaturity there. I knew what he wanted me to see in the first five minutes. He spent the next twenty-five beating me over the head with it."

"Fascinating."

I'm not making this up. Jansen starred in a movie ten years ago that was savaged because it felt more like a lecture than a story. It was called *Room 116*, about a guy who's lying in a hospital bed (in Room 116) dying slowly and in immense pain. And the doctors can't kill him 'cause it's against their creed or whatever. Jansen played his part well, but it's just scene after scene of this guy moaning in bed, and by the end of the movie it's like, okay, we get it, fucking kill him already. Anyway, that little spiel I just delivered was adapted from Ebert's review of that movie.

"But Matthew's a talented director," I add, because I don't want Wittig to think I'm one of those people who hate everything. And I'm not. I like most things.

Strange music leeches through the door of Matthew the director's apartment. It's this highly danceable music with this guy speaking monotonously over a drumbeat and synthesizers. I can't tell what he's saying yet.

There's a note on the door: "Just come right in."

So we go right in, me following Wittig and feeling a little nervous but not quite as bad as you might think. The first and only time I went to the Lewis Barker Thompson Hardy Christmas party, I threw up in the bathroom as soon as I got to the restaurant. I hate stuff like that. Social engagements. Mingling. Finding that stride of charming superficiality. I just don't know what to say to people. I'm good for about a minute, but after that I'm unbearable. I'm just not that interesting. I mean, I wouldn't want to talk to me at a party.

But tonight is different.

Tonight, I am not me, and that is the greatest comfort in the world.

Find a place. In the park. Sit and watch the ducks. Watch the sky and turn around. I'll be there in your dream. Find a place. In the park. Sit and watch the ducks. Watch the sky and turn around. I'll be there in your dream.

That's what the monotone voice is saying. Over and over.

I like it. I don't know why.

It's a studio apartment, and people have crammed themselves between the walls like you wouldn't believe. There's way more people here than were at the play. I follow Wittig through the crowd, since he seems to know where he's going. The floor is hardwood, the ceiling high. Paintings, sculptures abound. If I were the kind of person who used words like *chic*, I'd say this is a very chic apartment.

The back wall consists of windows, and they look out high above the city. People are standing outside on the balcony as well, leaning against the railing, smoking cigarettes.

Wittig turns and says something to me, but I can't understand him. There must be a hundred people here. Like ants, most have assembled in the middle of the room. Bouncing. Gyrating. A colony of dancing. Others stand in the kitchen around the stove island. Or sit on counters, or along the walls. Certainly this guy can't know everyone here. If I invited everyone I knew to a party, there'd be about eight people in the room, including my parents. All you can hear is a jumble of voices and above them—*find a place. In the park. Sit and watch the ducks…*

Next thing I know, we're standing in front of this guy garbed in black, with moussed black hair, black-framed glasses, who isn't even thirty, and Wittig's got his arm around my shoulder and he's saying, "Matt, I want you to meet a dear, dear friend of mine. I brought him to the show tonight. This is James Jansen. I think you've probably seen his work."

Right off, I don't like this kid. He's impressed to meet me, it's obvious, because for three seconds his mouth hangs open and he doesn't, or can't, speak. I mean, James Jansen is standing in his house, you know? But then he catches himself and gets this cool, smug look on his face that I'd like to peel right off. He's not honest, and I don't respect that. It's okay to be blown away that I'm standing here. That I took time out of my important, maniacally busy life to come to your weird fucking play.

I thrust my hand forward. "Jim," I say, real understated-like.

"Matt." He shakes my hand, then looks at Wittig and breaks. "You brought James fucking Jansen to my show?" He releases my hand and hugs Wittig. Okay, now he's coming around. Kid might be all right. But if I were a lesser Star, you can tell he'd try to come off like it was no big deal.

"Guys want a drink?" Matt offers.

"I'd like one of those with Tanqueray." Wittig points to the martini in Matthew's hand, "and Jim would like, I know this, hold on…a double Absolut with one cube of ice, no lime."

Matthew threads his way to the open bar. A spinning disco ball dangles from the ceiling, its radials of light causing the liquor bottles to flicker intermittently.

He returns with our drinks, and I really wish Jansen liked cranberry juice or something, because I can't stomach downing another glass of vodka.

"It's too fucking loud in here!" Matthew shouts over the music, like he's annoyed he has enough friends to fill an apartment. "Let's step outside!"

I barely sip the vodka, but by the time we push through the horde of dancers and reach the glass doors, I can feel the alcohol behind my eyes.

When we step outside, I try not to act too enthralled, but man the city is stunning tonight. We're thirty-nine floors up and the breeze is gentle and mild. The three of us find a place on the railing, and we stand there just gazing out over the sweep of light and motion and sound far below. I'm damn near in tears, but like I said,

I don't show it. You've got to figure Jansen's experienced far more beauty than some off-off Broadway director's balcony.

Wittig's standing between us and he puts his arms around the both of us.

"Gentlemen," he says, "what a night, huh?"

Matt and I don't say anything, because what are you going to say? I think he's being rhetorical.

"Matt, it came off even better than I thought it would," Wittig continues.

"Even the scenes with the therapist? You know, I've had concerns they're too chauvinistic."

"Especially those. They're the make-or-break scenes of your play, and they make it. You really pulled it off." Wittig takes a big sip of his martini, really pounding down the gin.

"I appreciate you saying that, Paul."

"I mean you really, really pulled it off. Really."

Wittig's sloshed. He's getting ready to say something else, but then notices his martini glass is empty.

"Gentlemen, I'm going for a refill. I shall return."

Wittig walks back into the party and Matt watches him go, shaking his head.

"He was my advisor at Columbia."

"He was bragging on you tonight before the show."

"Was he now."

"He a playwright, too?"

"He wrote a masterpiece when he was twenty-four called *In the Can*. I don't know if you've heard of it. He doesn't write much now. But he's brilliant. Look, I really appreciate you coming. It's not typical theatre."

"You made me think, and not much does these days."

God, I hope he doesn't ask me anything else about the play. I really feel bad for hating it.

Matt leans over the railing and spits. On the other end of the balcony, I notice these two women stealing glances at me. They're both wearing highly glittery dresses, and on closer inspection, I see that they're twins: beautiful, brunette twins. I flash my best Jansen smile and turn back to Matt.

"Say, Matt?"

"Yeah?"

"Reason I'm in New York is I'm doing research for an upcoming part. I'm going to play an actor in the off-Broadway scene. And I've never worked here. Always done film. So there's a lot I don't know. And of course to do a character right, I've got to really understand where they're coming from."

"Sure."

I sip my vodka. It's growing on me.

"So I was wondering if I could talk to you about your experience. Not tonight of course, since you've got your party here, but maybe this week. And I'd love to meet the actors from *Love in the 0's*, get a window into their lives."

"Hell, Jim, I'll put you in my play if you want."

"Really?"

"Look, while *Love in the 0's* runs in Hamilton, it's a work in progress. I've written a few dozen scenes that could potentially work. The story'll stay the same. It'll stay a half-hour long, but I'm experimenting with what best depicts the course of this relationship. In fact, I can think of a scene right now that would be perfect for you. And I'd love to see how it plays in front of a crowd."

"What's the part?"

Matt polishes off the rest of his martini.

"You'd play the shrink. I wrote two parts. One for a man, one for a woman, which you saw tonight. Despite what Paul says, I'm not sure a woman shrink is the best thing for the play. You be interested?"

"Absolutely."

That puts a hell of a smile across his face.

I take the last sip of vodka. I could breathe fire.

"If I give you a script before you leave tonight, could you come read tomorrow?"

Of course I can, but I grimace because Stars never have time to do anything.

"What time?"

"Two? I'd do it earlier, but I'm going to feel pretty shitty tomorrow morning."

I pause for no real reason.

"All right."

"Since it's a short scene, what I'm thinking is, if we nail it fast, which I'm sure we will, we could be ready to show it by next performance, which is Thursday. That's perfect, don't you think? You get firsthand experience doing theatre in New York. I get to work with one of the greatest actors of the last twenty years. It's a fucking dream, Jim."

He's pretty happy now. I think it's starting to hit him that he's recruiting James Jansen for his shitty play.

"You need another drink, Jim." He takes my glass before I can argue and walks back inside.

Now only the twins and I share the balcony.

I look over at them and smile again.

"Evening, ladies."

They smile back, far younger than I first thought. Hardly twenty.

One of them says, "Could you help us settle a bet?"

Everything is buzzing. This may be the best I've felt my whole life. I step toward them. Champagne and strawberries on their breaths.

"My sister, Dawn, says you're that movie star, James Jansen. But I don't think you are. I think you just look like him. Who's right? I got twenty bucks riding on this."

"You're right," I say, giving her this soul-penetrating stare.

"So you aren't him?"

"Nope." But I say it like I don't mean it. Real flirtatious-like. She laughs and sips her champagne. "You're pretty cute in person."

"What? You don't believe me?"

She steps closer and her sister comes around the other side so they've got me backed up against the railing.

"We had another bet," Dawn says.

"What's that?"

"I bet Heather a hundred dollars you'd come home with us. You wouldn't let me lose that money, would you?"

"I'd hate to cost you money," I say. And I would. Man, these women smell good.

"All right, stand aside." Matt reaches a hand between the twins and I take my glass of vodka.

"Do we know each other?" he asks, looking at Heather and then Dawn. He doesn't say it meanly, and I guess it's a reasonable question. Heather and Dawn glance at each other, and I wonder if they're communicating in some special twin way. Matt looks at me.

"Everything cool, Jim?"

"Aces."

He smiles that oh-I-know-what-you're-up-to smile. And he's right. I am up to it.

"Oh to be you. Well, then. I'll leave you three. Jim, come find me before you leave, and I'll give you that script." He winks at me and walks inside, and before my attention turns back to the women, I get to wondering whatever happened to Wittig. Scanning the dim, flashy living room, music pumping through the glass, I finally see him: a short, tweed-suit sporting, gray-bearded man, martini glass raised, in the thick of that dancing colony, sandwiched between two tall, slim men.

Chapter 5

his caterpillar ~ why they can't stay at the Waldorf ~ the triangle of goodness ~ the joy of twins ~ the contents of their refrigerator ~ doesn't even say goodbye ~ the diner called DINER ~ it's all chemicals ~ studies his lines ~ Dr. Lovejoy

Four years ago, I carved a deep gash into my chin with a razor. On purpose. It bled for six hours before I realized I needed stitches. It took four to close the wound, but I got what I wanted—a quarter-inch scar on the left side of my chin nearly identical to the one on Jansen's.

It looks like the footprint of an eight-legged caterpillar now, and the twin with short hair is touching it as we sit in the backseat of a cab, en route to their pad, as they call it.

"That is the most precious little scar I've ever seen," she says. "Look at this, Dawn."

"Oh God, that's cute. How'd it happen?"

FAMOUS

"I walked into the corner of a car door on the set of *Greener Grass*."

These women can't keep their hands off me. I'm sitting in the middle of the backseat, one on either side of me, focusing on their luxurious smell rather than the cab funk.

"Where the fuck are you going, dude?" Dawn yells at the cabby. "I said East Thirty-Seventh and Lexington—"

"We go there."

"You're taking the long way. I want the short way. You're out of your mind if you think I'm paying the scenic route fare."

"What is scenic route?"

"Unbelievable," Dawn mutters. "He knows exactly what he's doing. We aren't fucking tourists here!"

Heather places her right hand on my cheek and turns my face toward hers. Of the two, she has sweeter eyes.

"Baby, why can't we stay at your pad tonight? I know you must be shacked-up in some killer suite."

"I'd love to," I say. "I really would. But I'm here with my girlfriend. Now she expects me not to come home. That's all right. But showing up with two buxom ladies like yourselves would get me thrown out on my ass. You understand."

"Shit, I'd sleep in Central Park if it was with you."

Heather and Dawn live in a two bedroom apartment in Murray Hill. I have a hunch they're models, but I don't ask. I mean, they have to be, right? How do two twenty-year-olds afford a place in Manhattan?

It's 1:15 in the morning when we step out of the elevator onto their floor. The building is dead silent. I'm walking behind them, and they keep looking back at me with these wicked grins. I know it should've occurred to me long before now, but it hits me suddenly that we're probably going into their apartment to be naughty. And my head's spinning so much from this wonderful, inconceivable day which began more than eighteen hours ago, that I can't even assess whether or not I'm ready to live out this fantasy. I'm not a terribly sexual person in real life. There are guys out there, who I'm sure think about it much more than me. I don't even look at that much porn. I've only slept with one person in my entire life—this nice girl I dated my freshman year in college, when it still looked like I might turn out like everyone else.

So as Heather unlocks the door to their apartment and we stroll inside, I'm kind of wondering whether I'm up to this.

Man, these women must be in love with themselves. When the lights flick on, I notice that the living room walls are adorned with enlarged photographs of Heather and Dawn. The one over the couch is a photo of one of them (can't tell which), in a cowboy hat, sitting bareback on a very lucky horse, and looking sultrily into the camera. Over the flatscreen, they've hung a collage of all the magazine covers they've appeared on.

"Thought I recognized you two," I say as my eyes pass over the collage. I don't really recognize them. Just being nice. "Been in the city long?" I ask, moving through the living room and to the window which peers out over the fire escape and into another apartment building. Through an open window, I see the red digits of an alarm clock in a bedroom. I'm sure a couple sleeps somewhere in that blue darkness, and for some reason, the thought of this makes my chest ache for half a second.

"Nine months," one of them says, answering my question. They've disappeared into the kitchen, and I hear ice cubes dropping into glassware.

When they return to the living room, Dawn takes my jacket and Heather hands me a glass of bronze liquor.

"Hope you like scotch," she says. "Best thing we got."

I sip it. Tastes rotten and fiery, in a good way.

"It's fine." When you're famous, people open the good stuff.

"You've got a nice place here," I say.

Heather walks over to the window and takes my hand. She leads me back to the couch, and the three of us sit down with our drinks. I'm nervous, but the scotch is helping. These girls are so gorgeous. Almost too gorgeous. If you saw them from a distance, you'd think they were sophisticated, too, but sitting here beside them, I see they aren't. I'm not saying they're stupid or anything. Just not as deep as I first thought. Maybe because they're young. I guess everybody you meet is eventually a letdown.

"How old are you?" I ask.

"Twenty," Heather says. "How old are you?"

"Thirty-eight." Shit. Jansen's thirty-nine. But I don't think they know that.

Heather begins to run her fingers through my hair. They're both looking at me sort of funny, and you can tell they don't really want to talk.

My scotch is gone.

"How does it feel?" Dawn asks me while Heather touches the cool tip of her nose against my cheek.

"How does what feel?"

"Out of that entire crowd of scrumptious men, we picked you." She brushes her hair behind her shoulders and tilts her head, waiting my reply. Her dress glitters, rose and gold.

"You do this often? Is this your thing? Finding guys at parties and bringing them home with you?"

"It's not like we're whores," Dawn says.

"I don't think he means that," Heather defends. "Jim, when we see a guy we both like, we bring them home and make them feel good and let them make us feel good and make each other feel good. It's a triangle of goodness. You see anything wrong with that?"

"No." Feeling pretty aroused now.

Heather nibbles my ear and stands. "Come on."

I follow the twins into their bedroom. Feel like I'm straddling this fence, and on one side is fear, on the other, pure sensuality. They sort of go hand in hand I think.

"Ladies," I say as we enter the dark bedroom, and Dawn lights three candles on a dresser and turns on a lava lamp. "I know you probably think I do this all the time, but I've never had two. I just don't—"

"We'll take care of you, baby," Heather says as the bite of the struck match fills the room, and I kind of love her for saying that.

They step out of their glittery dresses and climb onto the bed. They're naked in the candlelight, on their knees facing each other. Long hair. Short hair. Miles of smooth skin. Like one creature. More beauty than I have ever seen. They hold hands. The comforter is black silk. They begin to kiss, and then wave me over to join them.

This moment, this night is so much more than Lance deserves. As I undress, I can feel him beginning to fade. I won't fight it. I think I'm beginning to understand now.

Some things, you just let die.

In the morning, I climb out of bed before they wake and walk into the kitchen, fully intending to prepare a breakfast of historic proportions. But when I open the fridge, I see that this is not in the cards. There's a bag of lettuce, several dozen bottled waters, and more Yoplait than any human being should ever see at one time.

I open the freezer, praying for a bag of bagels, something, but it houses only trays of ice and frozen dinners. Low-fat, no salt, low-calorie, cholesterol-free, organic, soy, vegan meals, to be specific.

My head feels like a bowling ball on my shoulders, and yogurt isn't going to remedy this hangover. I walk back into the twins' bedroom. They look lovely curled up back-to-back, and I stand there for a moment, just taking them in. I couldn't do this if they were awake, because last night is over. Last night wasn't about a connection, or liking, or loving. It's awfully sad, and I'm doing all I can not to give a shit, but that's difficult for me. So I stand at the foot of their bed for five minutes, watching them sleep, loving them as much as one can when under the gun of these callous rules.

Then I take my horribly wrinkled clothes out into the living room and dress. I'll need to get my suit pressed before I go anywhere important. It's 8:10, and I've got to have some coffee, something greasy.

I don't even leave a note.

So it's 8:30 and I'm strolling down the sidewalk, and I'll bet everyone who walks past me is thinking, man that guy had a big night. And I did. It's true. My suit looks like shit, and I've got these dark sunglasses on, a script under my arm, and even though I feel pretty rundown, I'm floating.

I cross E. 40th Street, and there's a diner on the corner called DINER, so I step inside and claim a stool. I go ahead and take the sunglasses off so people don't think I'm an asshole. It's okay to wear them outside at this hour of the morning if you're a Star, but inside might be pushing it.

I order so much damn food it takes up more than my allotment of counter space, but who gives a fuck, you know? I'm just in that kind of a mood this morning, and that's pretty rare for me. Normally, I'm highly concerned about what people think. Even strangers.

I'm not used to being this happy, and I can't imagine it lasting all day. If I'm still this high in ten hours, I'll be hurting, like at the end of an orgasm when it all becomes too much. You know, it's kind of sad being this happy, because it can't last. And the second you realize that, the joy begins to wane. And once you start coming down, you wonder if you were really happy at all, because shouldn't real happiness withstand the knowledge that it can't last? And once you realize you weren't really happy, it occurs to you that what caused this interval of euphoria was nothing more than a bunch of chemicals floating around in your brain.

Fuck me. I've talked myself out of being happy.

When I finish the short stack and the bacon, I get my coffee refilled and pull out the script. It's only a twenty-eight page play. My lines begin on page fifteen and end on seventeen. Matt's gone to the trouble of bolding them for me.

As it turns out, my character is a therapist—the absolute worst therapist you've ever met in your life. And in my scene, Gerald brings Cindy (they're the main characters in the play) to have a session with me because Cindy has mistreated the love of Gerald's life—his dog, Poopsie.

I'm Dr. Lovejoy, and the scene goes like this:

```
ACT ONE

SCENE FIVE

AT RISE:

The following morning. GERALD and
CINDY are sitting beside each other
on a loveseat, alone in the office of a
psychiatrist, DR. LOVEJOY. DR. LOVEJOY
walks in and sits down in a chair
before the couple. GERALD is visibly
upset.

            GERALD
    Thank you for seeing us on such
    short notice, Dr. Lovejoy.
            DR. LOVEJOY
```
Yes, well, my time is extremely limited, so why don't you tell me the problem.
```
            CINDY
            (sarcastically)
    I'm the problem.
            DR. LOVEJOY
```
I'll decide that.

GERALD

No, she's right, Doctor. She most certainly is the problem. She's an enormous problem.

DR. LOVEJOY

(to Gerald)

So. You initiated this session. What would you like for me to say?

GERALD

What do you mean?

DR. LOVEJOY

What did you come here to hear? Everyone who comes into this office has something in mind they want to hear. Some behavior they want rationalized. Permission to cheat on their wife. Write off their parents. What is it that you want?

GERALD

I want you to help us to—

DR. LOVEJOY

(standing and shouting)

Just stop! Let us dispense with you trying to make me think you really care about having this relationship healed. Let's go right to the end of where all of this is going. What do

you want? Permission to leave her? Go ahead. Leave. You want to change her. Knock yourself out. I don't care. Just tell me what you want to hear, and I'll say it convincingly and sympathetically, and give you my bill and you can go ahead and do what you were already going to do, with my four hundred and twenty-five dollar-an-hour blessing. So, Gerald. What. Do. You. Want. To. Hear.

>GERALD
>
>(tearing up)

Last week, Cindy microwaved my dog, Poopsie, for forty-five seconds. It didn't kill her, but she walks diagonally now. I want to microwave Cindy's Persian cat.

>DR. LOVEJOY
>
>(sits back down and leans forward, looking intently at CINDY and GERALD)

Ready?

BLACKOUT

Chapter 6

returns to Edenwald ~ in Central Park ~ oops ~ rehearsal ~ tries to act ~ fails ~ has an epiphany

After the night I've had, it's a bit of a letdown returning to the Worst Hotel in the World. It's nearly 11:00 a.m., and the sun already showering through the blinds. I can tell it's going to be another blistering day. Laughter reaches me through the cracked window, and I stand peering through the blinds for a moment, watching the boys throwing dice down on the baking concrete steps of their apartment building. I wonder if they do this all summer long.

It feels terrible to be here, like a great, fat lie, so I change into a pair of khaki slacks and a white oxford shirt and get the hell out of this rank hotel.

Since I still have several hours before I have to be at Hamilton Studio, I catch a cab to W. 110 St., the northern boundary of Central Park, and follow a path until the smell of trees is stronger than the smell of traffic.

I wander off the path and find a place in the shade of a big oak. The grass is soft and warm. Through the foliage, I see pieces of blue, spring sky, and I smile at that joy swells up in me again.

I take the script out of my satchel and read through my lines once more. I'd be lying if I said I wasn't a little scared. Matt's expecting an Oscar winner to pull off this scene in his play. Jansen's a terrific actor. Sure, he does his share of suspense flicks that don't call for the nuances of brilliant acting. But he's also put out five or six Oscar-caliber performances, and it's these against which I'll be judged.

I've got my lines down cold, so I'm not worried about forgetting them. My memory is photogenic. What I'm worried about is me reading onstage with the other actors, and Matt and everyone in the theatre knowing instantly that I've never acted professionally in my life. I have the physical resemblance to Jansen to pull this off, and I can do his voice. But what concerns me is not knowing if I have the hardwiring to play this part. Sure I've said Jansen's famous lines to myself in the mirror while shaving, and I thought I was pretty good. But honestly, what do *I* know?

I eat lunch at a Greek deli on Central Park N. Rehearsal is only an hour away, and my mouth runs dry just thinking about it. As I'm standing to leave, this woman saunters over to my table and says, "I'm sorry to bother you, Mr. Jansen, but could I trouble you for an autograph? I'm a huge fan." She hands me a pen and a credit card receipt to sign.

"What's your name?" I ask, turning the receipt over on my table.

"Lauren. I just loved you in *My Last Day*."

I sign, "To Lauren," but I can't really think of anything remotely witty or charming to write. So I just sign my name, hand it back to her.

On my way out the door, I realize that I signed Lancelot Blue Dunkquist.

I hate that fucking name.

I arrive at Hamilton Studio at 2:05 and walk through the lobby into the theatre. It's dark and empty except for the stage, where the director and two stars sit on the sofa set-piece, basking under that autumn-afternoon lighting.

I've never been in a theatre quite like this. Well, I've never been in *any* theatre since I did *Thoroughly Modern Millie* in middle school, so I guess that doesn't mean anything. The stage is the low point of the room. Seats surround it on three sides, each row a little higher than the one in front of it. For *Love in the 0's*, the stage consists of several hardwood panels that jut out from the back wall. There's no curtain. Set pieces are swapped out under the cover of darkness.

"Jim!" Matt calls from the sofa as I descend toward the stage between the rows. He rises, along with his actors, and we meet at the foot of the first hardwood floor panel.

He's still dressed in black. I wonder if he's one of those people, who, once they find a cool outfit, stick with it until the end of time.

"Good to see you again, man," he says, sounding genuinely happy to see me. "I want to introduce you to Jane Remfry and Ben Lardner." The actors look to be in their mid-twenties. I wonder if they were in grad school with Matt. Ben is tall and quirky-looking. He has a goatee, and I've never cared for people who keep goatees. They're suspect.

"Ben, Jane," I say, shaking their hands. "A pleasure."

I'm turning it on now. I can feel Jansen flowing through me like a shot of adrenaline.

"I am so honored and excited to be working with you, Mr. Jansen," Jane says.

She's a cutie. Tall and slim. Short, blond hair. Very Icelandic.

"Call me Jim, please."

"I feel the same way, sir," Ben says, and he actually shakes my hand again which is pretty funny. They're star-struck as hell.

"So," Matt says, putting his hand on my shoulder, and grinning at me through those thick, black frames. "How'd things go for *you* last night after the party?"

I smile that I-slept-with-beautiful-twins smile, and he fills the empty theatre with his laughter.

"Let's do a scene, shall we?"

I follow everyone up onto the stage.

There's a brown leather loveseat, and Ben and Jane sit down.

There's a desk with a little lamp and a scattering of books and papers.

I sit on the edge of the desk.

"So, Jim, you've read the scene?"

"Several times."

Boy, my mouth's dry, my heart pumping like a piston.

"You off-book, yet?"

I don't know what that means.

"Yeah."

"Great. So, how about this?" Matt comes and sits on the desk beside me. When he speaks, he's highly expressive with his hands. "I'll tell you sort of what I'm thinking for this scene, and if you see it differently or there's something else you want to try, I'm totally open to that. I really want you to follow your instinct here, because that's what's going to make this scene great." He hops down. "I know the script says you walk in and sit down at rise, but when the lights come up I want everyone already sitting."

"Okay."

"Why don't you take a seat behind the desk."

I walk around to the swivel chair and sit down. My hands tremble now. I set my satchel on the floor, pull the script out, place it on the desk. Training wheels, just in case I blank.

Matt stands between the loveseat and the desk. I feel that light shining down on me from the blackness of the ceiling. Jane and Ben look so comfortable. I keep reminding myself of that quote I heard somewhere, that if you're scared, you should pretend like you're at ease, and no one will know.

"Everything," Matt says to all of us, "hinges on this scene."

Great. I'm going to fuck up this guy's play.

"I know," he continues, "there's this temptation to take it over the top here, and some directors would probably go for that, but I don't think we need to. The play itself, the way it treats relationships, is already so over the top, the acting shouldn't mimic that, you know?"

I most certainly do not know what in the hell he's talking about.

"Lookit, there's comedy here, but fuck up the timing, you know? This isn't Neil Simon. I want people to laugh, but not too much. The goal, honestly, is to unnerve them. They'll laugh for the same reason people laugh at funerals. So," he glances back at me, "want to give it a go?"

Oh God.

"Why not?"

What is my first line? Shit.

Matt walks off the stage and takes a seat in the first row.

"Let's do the whole scene," he says, "and I swear I won't interrupt you the first time. I'll just go ahead and tell you, Jim, I'm pretty bad about that. I mean, I could work on thirty seconds of dialogue for a whole afternoon. But I don't think we're going to have that problem today. Ben, whenever you're ready."

Ben takes a deep breath and stares for a moment into the floor.

When his eyes come back to mine, he's a different person. Vulnerable, wounded.

"Thank you for seeing us on such short notice, Dr. Lovejoy," he says gravely.

My line. Fuck. I lean forward and glance at page fifteen of the script.

"Yes, well. My time is extremely. Limited so why don't you tell me the problem."

That was awful. Wooden. Perfunctory.

"I'm the problem," Jane says, crossing her arms and glancing with annoyance into the empty theatre. She really looks pissed.

"I'll decide that."

"No, she's right, Doctor. She most certainly is the problem. She's an enormous problem." Ben is so good. I feel like he's really speaking to me.

My lines have evaporated. I grab the script.

"Sorry, Matt."

"It's all right. Stay with it."

"So," I continue, and I know it, everyone in the theatre knows it—I am dying up here. "You initiated this session what would you like for me to say?"

"What do you mean?"

"What did you come—"

"Okay!" Matt yells, coming out of his seat, "I know I said I wouldn't, but I want to stop here for a second." He walks onstage, begins pacing between the sofa and the desk.

"I think I know what you're up to here, Jim."

Man, I wish someone would dim those overhead lights. I'm sweating like a maniac.

"I don't think the whole acting like you can't act thing is going to work for this scene, and I'll tell you why. Don't get me wrong—it's frighteningly convincing. But like I said before, it's way, way over the top, and if this play gets any goofier, it'll fall apart. You know what I'm saying, Jim?"

"Absolutely."

Matt approaches me. "I think it might help if we get you out from behind this desk. Connect you to Gerald and Cynthia a little more. Here," he comes over, "let's slide your chair out to center stage."

This is dynamite. Now I'm sitting six feet away from Jane and Ben, and they're going to see the fear dripping from my face. My inability is so fucking glaring, I'm on the verge of running the hell out of this theatre right now.

"And Jim?" Matt says as he walks back to his chair on the front row, "let's slow things down a little. Feels like you're rushing your lines a tad."

Jane gives me a reassuring smile. Ben's looking up into the lighting grid. I wonder if they're embarrassed for me.

"Thank you for seeing us on such short notice, Dr. Lovejoy," Ben says, beginning the scene again.

"Yes. Well. My time is extremely limited…" I stop. If I don't take control of this situation immediately, I may lose everything. I begin to shake my head. Then I stand and look at Matt.

"I'm sorry, but I strongly disagree with you here. Look, you've written a cutting edge play. There's no doubt about that. And what is it you told me earlier that your goal was? To unnerve people. Right?"

An uneasy nod.

"What is more unnerving and uncomfortable than watching someone onstage who is totally dying? They're trying so hard, but they're forgetting lines, rushing lines, overacting. Mumbling. Trembling even. It's painful to watch, but it's also funny. Isn't that the juxtaposition you're going for? Uneasy laughter? What better captures that than a character who comes on stage before a few hundred people, and everyone's thinking 'is he acting like this on purpose'? Honestly? You tell me."

"I see what you're saying, Jim, I do, but—"

"But what? It's staring you right in the face, Matt. You told me to go with my instinct. 'That's what's going to make this scene great.' Didn't you say that?"

"Yeah."

"Well, my instinct is screaming at me, and this doesn't happen often, but I know in my gut, that this is how I should play this scene. Don't you feel it? We've had an epiphany here." I look at Jane. "Do *you* feel it?"

"Maybe. Yeah. I think I do."

"Ben?"

"It's his show, man."

"Well, I feel it, Matt," I say, stepping down toward him onto the next panel. "I feel it in my bones, man."

Matt removes his glasses and squeezes the bridge of his nose between his eyes.

"So what you're telling me," he says, "is you want to do this scene like you can't act? That's what you're saying?"

"That's what I'm saying."

"Do they pretend they can't act either?" he asks, pointing at Jane and Ben.

"No, just me. Otherwise, the audience would know. They carry on just like in the previous scenes."

"You're sure about this?"

I've won an Oscar, asshole.

"Absolutely."

Matt stands and stares at me sort of dumbfounded. He glances up at the lighting grid, at the sofa where his stars sit, at the desk, like he's taking his whole production in once last time before I royally fuck it all up.

When his eyes come back to mine, he shrugs, says, "All right, Jim. All right. Hell, that's why we're at Hamilton. To try shit out."

He walks back to his seat, sits down, crosses his legs.

"Let's run it again."

Chapter 7

Manta ~ eavesdrops on the graduates ~ watches the eel ~ Henry's ~ "Twice as Deep" ~ the beauty of Corey Mustin ~ like a demon in the house of God

Though the sun has long since descended beneath the metallic range of towers, when I step out of Hamilton Studio, the hot air engulfs me like a waft of furnace heat. The sidewalk brims with the Village night crowd—perfumed, elegant creatures, breezing past en route to food and drink and entertainment. I walk with them. It's 7:30, and I'm famished.

There's a Thai restaurant up ahead. I step inside. Very trendy. Very hip. Since I'm alone, the maître d' promises she can get me seated in fifteen minutes. I can't quite tell if she recognizes me, so I don't push it. Besides, you think Jansen has ever dined alone?

It's insanely loud. I make my way between tables to the crowded bar. When the bartender asks me what I'd like, I order Jansen's specialty without even considering it. I've worked hard today. A drink is very much in order.

The restaurant is called Manta, and it's filled with aquariums. There's one behind the bar teaming with these swollen goldfish that look like they've been puffed up and deformed by gamma radiation or something. Sitting in my barstool, I sip the Absolut and watch them drift lazily through the bright blue water.

I glance over at a staircase, where a tiny waitress carries two monstrous trays up the steps to the second level. I know it's sort of mean, but it'd be funny as hell if she took a tumble with all of that food.

The maitre d' returns and I follow her across the room to this other bar which backs up against an enormously long aquarium. All of the stools are occupied except for one. She seats me, leaves a menu. I glance down the bar at my tablemates. Most have books open beside their steaming plates, and a sort of concentration in their eyes which precludes engagement.

After the waiter brings me a glass of water and takes my order, I pull out the script and bury myself in my lines. I won't have this safety net tomorrow night. It knots my stomach just thinking about the performance. Matt's nervous, too, doubting whether he should let me go the acting-like-you-can't-act route. But it's a done deal, because that's the only route I know. I keep telling myself I have no reason to be nervous, because the worse I am, the more uncomfortable I appear to the audience, the better it will be.

The peanut chicken is good and spicy as hell. I spend most of my meal sucking on ice cubes, trying to quell the fire on my tongue. There's a table directly behind me, and everyone's having a terrific time. From what I can gather, they all attend NYU, and they're graduating this coming weekend. It's four guys and three girls, and they can't stop laughing about this time one of them "blew chunks" all over an English professor after a hard night of partying.

Man, they're happy. They keep saying things like "Dude, I was so fucking wasted!" and "yeah, but we only hooked up that first night in Nassau" and "totally, we'll like totally hook it up." And they really seem to enjoy saying fuck. But that's understandable. It's a fun, versatile word.

What's most interesting about this group, is they're all business majors, so they're going on to law school or grad school or into the workplace. And you can tell they think they're very well-adjusted, since they're not only exceptional students, but "know how to party." They'd probably describe themselves as intelligent professionals by day, and wild, clubbing maniacs by night. I suppose they think that juxtaposition makes them interesting, which is fairly sad, because if you were sitting here listening to them, it'd take you all of five seconds to conclude they're the dullest young people you've ever seen. That constant laughter doesn't fool me. But they don't know they aren't interesting yet. That realization will be along in about five years.

After they leave, I put away my script and just sit there with a cup of black coffee, mesmerized, because on this end of the aquarium, a moray eel moves ribbon-like through the teal, glowing water. With a huge, birdlike head and these terrifying teeth, he glides openmouthed through his section of the tank, restlessly circling the same rock, and watching me through beady, reptilian eyes.

When I leave Manta, it's only 9:00 p.m., so I don't feel much like returning to my Bronx hotel. I walk up 2nd

Ave. for a long, long time, not really conscious of anything except the underlying murmur of the city.

A few blocks north of Stuyvesant Square, I pass the door of a club called Henry's. The Blues pours from the open doorway, and I hear the crowd applauding the moaning of a guitar. I've gone nearly to the end of the block when I turn around. Returning to the door, I shell out the twelve-dollar cover charge and enter the smoky room.

It's loud as hell. I don't really want a drink, so I don't bother with the line to reach the bar in back. Instead, I squeeze my way through the crowd, until I spot a recently-vacated table in a corner. The martini and shotglasses have yet to be cleared, but I don't mind. I hang my jacket on a chair and take a seat.

The club is small. Posters of famous musicians adorn the walls, and the stage is well-lit and lined with enormous speakers aimed at the audience. It's the kind of place that's so dark, you don't even notice who else is in the room. Just you and the band.

Man, this guy is just wailing on his guitar, and what's interesting, is he's as far from the epitome of a blues guitarist as you can imagine. He looks like a computer engineer—thin, tall, silver-framed glasses, smooth-faced, and dressed like someone who has never given a thought to style in their life. We're talking blue jeans, tennis shoes, and a white, sweat-soaked tee-shirt. You'd probably think that he had the voice of a timid, fourteen-year-old boy, but when he finishes his guitar solo and steps back toward the mic, what springs from his mouth is the grittiest, wisest, most mournful crooning I've ever heard.

The song is apparently called "Twice as Deep," and he sings this chorus over and over:

"I put you in the ground
but you crawled back out
You been hauntin' me, baby
You been spookin' me, baby
I'm a ghost, too, but I gotta sleep
Next time I'll bury you twice as deep."

When the song's over, he introduces the drummer and the bass player.

"And I'm Corey Mustin," he says, "and we're going to play the Blues for you all night. Two, three, four…"

They rip into another song, this one slower, softer, sadder. It's about how he's been so lonely since he moved to New York, and I wonder if the song is really autobiographical. By the middle of the song, I'm feeling pretty sorry for the guy. He sings with his eyes closed, like he doesn't care if everyone knows what's in his heart.

"I ain't seen a soul
Since I got off the bus
Who smiled like they smile back home
I been wanderin' the streets
Cause I got no friend
And I can't stop thinking about home
I drink through the nights
And sleep through the days
Can't take much more on my own
A man needs a woman
A man needs a friend
But all I've got is this gun."

Man, I like the Blues. Corey Mustin breaks into another solo, and I settle back into the chair and just watch him go, his fingers sliding up and down the neck of the guitar like they were designed for nothing else.

And the look on the guy's face while he plays is something you so rarely see these days—purposeful, not a glimmer of self-consciousness, pure fluidity, unselfishly doing what he was put here to do.

And as I sit here watching him play, I start feeling kind of sad, and what makes me sad is how beautiful Corey Mustin is on stage. His talent is a glimpse of truth. It touches me like nothing I can remember. It unnerves me, too, and the only way I can describe it is to compare it to how demons must feel in the presence of God. He's beautiful. They know He's beautiful. But they hate Him because He's beautiful, because they're ugly and despicable, and nothing will ever change that.

I haven't been here ten minutes, but I stand up and push desperately through the crowd, tears welling in my eyes, beginning to spill down my face. He's singing that chorus again by the time I reach the door

"A man needs a woman,
a man needs a friend
but all I've got is this gun."

And as I step back out into the night, all I can think is fuck you Corey Mustin. I'd kill him if I met him on the street right now. I really would.

Chapter 8

rain ~ the acting workshop ~ warns of the hardships of Hollywood ~ the big night ~ into the black

I promised Wittig I'd come talk to one of his acting workshops on Thursday, but when I wake up in that disgusting bed, the only thing on my mind is that I'll be on stage in less than ten hours.

I slip into these olive slacks and a baize button-up, so I'm looking pretty sharp. Since I'm not supposed to be at Columbia until 11:00, I drag the chair over to the window and sit down.

It's raining for what must be the first time in days, so I crack the window and let the cool damp air filter into the room. Before long, I'm inundated with the smell of wet concrete and metal. The sound is all raindrop-pattering and tire-sloshing over wet streets.

Those dice-throwing boys must be indoors today. I wonder what games they play when it rains.

I walk into the classroom at five minutes past 11:00, and wait until I've shaken Wittig's hand to remove my sunglasses. It's the ultimate I-am-a-Star statement—wearing sunglasses on a rainy day. But, you know, people expect this sort of thing from me now, and I'm not in the business of letting them down.

I can tell you the class of fourteen students is pretty thrilled to meet me. Seven girls, seven boys, and they're all sitting on the hardwood floor along the wall. This isn't a normal classroom with chairs and a blackboard and all that educational jazz. For one thing, it's a very large room called a studio, with big, curved windows looking out on the misty campus. Pretty breathtaking actually. And there are props all over the place—chairs, couches, wooden cubes—that make the room look kind of like a playroom for college students.

After Wittig and I exchange pleasantries, he turns to his students and says, "I know you're all probably shocked, but I wanted this to be a surprise. I'm sure you already recognize him, but if not, it is my distinct pleasure to introduce you all to James Jansen. He's starred in more movies than I can count, many of which I'm sure you've all seen. He's been nominated four times for an Academy Award, and he won one ten years ago. He's been kind enough to come talk to you and maybe," he glances at me as he says this, and fuck was I afraid this might happen, "do some scene work with you. Jim, the class is yours."

Wittig takes a seat along the wall with his students, and I'm standing there in this big airy room, listening to the rain on the windows, and I don't have the first inkling of what to say.

"Can I get everyone's name?" I ask. "Starting at this end. And, in one sentence, why you want to be an actor."

"I'm Jonathan Moore, and I want to act, oh jeez, that's hard, let me think…because I love creating characters. Just getting into them, I mean."

"Jen Steele. Because I can't do anything else."

Everyone chuckles at this.

"Pete Meyers. I don't really know. I just do it."

More laughter.

"Anne Winters. I want to act because…"

While the fourteen students fumble for answers, I try to figure out what the hell I'm going to talk about, and by the time the last student bumbles through a heartfelt "I've always known ever since I was a little kid that I was meant to act," I've got an idea.

The room is quiet again. I walk over to a wooden cube and push it back across the room so I don't have to stand.

"It's wonderful to be here this morning," I say. "Now what I just asked you was sort of an unfair question, right?" Everyone sort of laughs nervously and agrees that it was. Man, when people are in awe of you, they hang on your every word. It's pretty cool.

"It's like asking a man why he loves his wife. In front of her. He just does. Why do you love to act? You just do. You can't necessarily express it, but that doesn't mean it's not the most important thing in your life.

"When Professor Wittig invited me to come talk to you, I was a little hesitant because I didn't know quite what I should say. I've been in this business a long time. Twenty-two years. And I've been mulling over all the experiences I've had, searching for something I can tell you about making it in the movie business. Been looking for some nugget of wisdom I can relate to you. Well, much to my surprise, I've found there's really only one thing I can say. I mean sure, I could stress the importance of not letting directors push you around, about choosing projects wisely, about not letting your head explode in the good times. But is that what you need to hear right now? No. This is what you need to hear right now. What you have to understand if you want to go all the way, and I'm assuming you all do. Otherwise you'd be in the real world right now.

"Well, this is it—it's a hard, hard, hard, hard business. And it is a business, and if you ever forget for one second that it's anything but, they'll send you packing. The bottom line is *not* digging into your characters, or mastering your emotions and being able to turn on the spigot at will. The bottom line is—can you make money for other people with your acting talent? That's it. If you can't, forget it. What you have to do is hone your craft and become so damn riveting that people pay—eagerly—to watch you on a screen or a stage.

"Let me tell you a hard truth. There are people in LA who don't give a remote shit about the craft. Here's a harder truth. They're brilliant actors. They make gobs of money. So what am I saying? Let's condense it to this. Care about your craft. Care more about making other people care about your craft. 'Cause let me tell you. You might be the best actor on the planet, but if you never get beyond theatre in the park, what does it matter? And don't say it matters to you and that's enough. Bullshit. Acting is more about what you give the audience than what you give yourself."

That's all I've got. And you know what? I made it up. A Lancelot original speech. Actually, that's not true. It's from Jansen's *Inside the Actors Studio* interview with James Lipton. But it *felt* like I made it up.

Since I get quiet for a minute, all the students sort of look at each other like "are we supposed to clap?" And even though I've probably ripped the hope right out of their chests, and they're ready to hang themselves, they clap for me! Wittig, too! He's beaming like I've just espoused a hard, honest truth that these students are going to take with them for the rest of their lives. I can't think about it too hard, or I'll start laughing.

When they finally stop clapping, I say, "I'd be happy to answer any questions you have."

Wittig butts in and tells his students, "Let's keep the questions on a useful level. Like technique and relaxation. Let's try to stay away from 'what's it like to be famous?' Okay?"

This very tall girl with long, straight black hair actually stands up and she blushes so deeply I think she's going to faint.

"I'm Natalie. Um…I'm sorry, Mr. Jansen, I'm just nervous."

"Oh, no, I'm more nervous than you are." It's true, too. I probably am.

Natalie smiles. She's so thin and pale I feel kind of sorry for her, so I give a real serious if-I-like-you-you-must-be-okay smile.

"Okay," she says, "I have a hard time getting out of myself when I do a part? It's like, when I watch these actors onscreen or onstage, I can just look at them and tell they're so engrossed in the part, and I see it when I watch you, too, so could you tell me how you do it? How you get into character so convincingly?"

"You always hear 'get out of yourself, get into the part.' Well, I disagree with that. When I'm doing an intense scene, the truth is, I'm usually thinking about myself. What I'm going to get at the grocery store next time, about some book I'm reading, what I want for lunch. I find it helpful *not* to think about the character I'm portraying, you know?" That, I did make up on the fly. "Confidence also helps," I say, and I suddenly have another great idea. "Tell you what, Natalie, let's do something. Do you have an audition monologue in your head?"

"Um, yeah."

"Let's hear it."

"Are you... Okay. Hold on. Oh my God."

"Stop. I'm not really serious. I just wanted to make a point. You're standing here, and if you had the sort of confidence I was talking about, it shouldn't have even crossed your mind not to do it. You should dive right in. Don't be scared. That's wasted brain power. It takes your attention away from doing the part effectively. So Natalie, everyone, don't wait for success to be confident. Go ahead and just believe in yourself right now. It'll make you a better actor, and it'll get you work."

I'm starting to enjoy this. You know, it wouldn't be that difficult to be a professor. You just say the same thing over and over, and when that gets old, ask questions. I could do this all day.

The lights will go down in less than fifteen minutes, and I feel deliriously happy. I'm sitting in the green room in my costume, a heavy brown wool suit and yellow bowtie, drumming my fingers against my knees and not even worrying over my lines.

Jane and Ben are sitting on the couch, Ben bitching about one of his roommates drinking his soy milk, Jane nodding attentively. I try to absorb their ease. I succeed. The greatest moment of my life so far is coming, and I'm ready for it.

"It's been a pleasure working with you two," I say, interrupting Ben.

They look over at me and smile.

Then I get up and head for the bathroom for one last pee.

When the lights come up, I'm sitting behind the desk, looking down the stage at Ben and Jane on the couch. The darkness beyond the stage is now full and alive. The play is sold out, the theatre packed. Time crawls by in chest-shuddering increments. I register the audience, know that suited men and perfumed women have paid money to come here and watch me, that Wittig and his students sit somewhere out in that audience darkness, anxious to receive the genius of my talent.

"Thank you for seeing us on such short notice, Dr. Lovejoy."

The air is buzzing. I can hear the blood in my brain. My line. My line. I can feel the audience collectively wondering why I'm not responding. How much time has passed since Ben spoke? My line. My line. I need to hear him say it again if I'm going to remember.

I clear my throat. It's so quiet. Above us, I hear those autumnal lights humming.

"Could we start over?" I ask.

God, my voice sounds strange in this theatre. Even through their masks of acting, the shock on the faces of Ben and Jane is unmistakable, their eyes widening in unison. In rehearsal, I said my lines with nervousness and imperfect timing, but I always said them. This is not how it was supposed to go. I'm too nervous to act nervous.

"Thank you for seeing us on such short notice, Dr. Lovejoy," Ben says again.

"Yes, well, my time's limited."

More silence.

Jane mouths something, but I can't decipher it.

I mouth back, "What?"

"Why don't you tell me the problem?" she mouths again.

"Why don't you tell me the problem?" I vocalize woodenly.

"I'm the problem," Jane says. I can't even remember her character's name.

Someone sneezes in the audience, and I look out into the darkness for the sneezer. My line. My line. My line. My chest is really heaving.

I smile that Jansen smile and stand. As I walk around the desk (not rehearsed either) Jane's still trying to mouth my lines to me, and boy does that make me angry.

"Cut that out," I say.

Her face goes white, and she eyeballs the floor. Ben turns red. I feel so lightheaded. Numb. I stop several feet from the couch and look down on them from my towering six foot, three-inch frame. I do not feel well.

I manage to turn and throw up on the stage instead of on Ben and Jane.

I wipe my mouth.

"Look at me," I say, and they do, and man you wouldn't believe how utterly mortified they are. I think they're more uncomfortable than I am.

I have to save this scene, so I blurt out the only thing that comes to mind.

"By God, you may walk out of here with that money, but which one of you is it going to be?"

Jane's eyes fill with tears.

The lights go down.

No.

I go down, my cheek against the hardwood floor.

The audience is gasping, the darkness spinning, voices calling that name which I covet.

Chapter 9

the night He won the Oscar ~ back in the green room ~ scares them with the threat of vomiting ~ makes an exit ~ going home ~ a hypothetical conversation between you and Lance (indulge him)

One of my best memories is watching James Jansen step onstage at the Academy Awards that early March evening ten years ago. He hadn't been picked to win the Oscar, but when they announced his name, the crowd roared and rose to its feet.

He won for his lead in a film called *Down From the Sleeping Trees*. Played this guy who's a junior in college when his father kills himself. What happens next is his mother freaks out and moves from Boston to this cabin in the North Carolina mountains, and Jansen, or his character I mean, drops out of school to help her. I won't say how it ends in case you haven't seen it, but it's genius. The actress who played his mother won an Oscar, too. *And* the movie got best picture. I've watched the tape of that Academy Awards at least once a week for the last five years. Sometimes, I even dress up and order in Chinese.

Anyway, he stepped onstage and gave the most gracious acceptance speech you've ever seen. Didn't even use a cheat sheet. And he was twenty-nine. Unreal.

Sometimes, when things aren't going too good, like now, I think about that night, and pretend I'm Jansen saying all those brilliant things to the crowd, just charming the hell out of everyone. You'd be surprised at how good it makes me feel. You really would.

I'm trying to do that now as I lie on the couch in the green room, but everyone's talking to me, Matt especially. He keeps asking what the fuck happened out there, and Wittig's in the room, too. I hear him talking to Ben, saying, "I just don't know. I just don't know."

Jane keeps asking when the ambulance is coming, and this stagehand is trying to shove a glass of water in my face.

All of the sudden, I get this very panicky feeling because of all the people around me and I say, very quietly and calmly, "Could everybody just leave me alone for a minute?"

But they don't hear me, because Matt asks me again what the fuck happened, and Wittig continues to tell Ben he just doesn't know.

"LEAVE ME ALONE!" I shout, and man does everybody shut up in a hurry.

Matt orders everyone out, even Ben and Jane and Wittig.

When it's just Matt and me, I sit up on the couch and lift the glass of water off the carpet and down the whole glass.

"I want to ask you something," Matt says. In (you guessed it) black again, he kneels down by the couch and stares at me through his black-framed glasses. I haven't been looked at like this since I left Charlotte. It makes me feel like Lance again, and I don't have to tell you how awful *that* feels.

"What just happened out there," he says.

"Well, I was standing there and—"

"I'm not asking you. I'm telling you. What happened out there was the most fucked-up piece of theatre I've ever seen. You froze."

"Stop right there." I hold out my hand, because if he says what I think he's going to say, I don't know what I'll do. "I think I'm going to puke," I say, and sort of make this highly regurgitative sound. Matt instantly backs off. I guess the fear of being vomited on pretty much trumps all.

"I'll be right back," I say, and I rush out of the room.

Everybody's lined up against the wall of dressing rooms, and before they can say anything, I mention how I'll be upchucking momentarily.

Since I don't know where the rear exit of Hamilton Studio is, I accidentally walk right out onto the stage as the dramaturge is telling the crowd how there's been a medical emergency and that I'm being ambulanced away as he speaks.

I walk right up the aisle between the most bewildered playgoers you've ever seen, and stop at the doors to the lobby. For some reason, I'm still not sure why, I turn around and face the audience, all of whom are looking at me. You can't tell me they aren't getting their money's worth tonight. Even my costars and the director and Wittig have come out onstage.

"Ladies and Gentlemen!" I shout at the top of my voice. Man, I feel strange. How often do you have the undivided attention of a hundred perplexed people? "Don't be alarmed! This is all part of the show!"

And with that I rush through the lobby and out the front doors, into a hard, warm rain.

A pessimist might say that tonight didn't go so well. And I'll be honest with you, the thought has crossed my mind. But as I walk through this wonderful rain, I have got to tell you, I don't feel so bad. I've been in New York just three days, and consider all I've done. Wittig, Matt's party, the model twins, landing this terrific acting gig, speaking to Wittig's class, my performance tonight. I'll tell you, I'm hard pressed not to smile right now. So I'm not a great actor. Who is really? We don't love actors. We love Stars. And being a Star has nothing to do with acting. It has to do with being recognizable. You're like a walking, breathing brand name. You bring comfort to people. Constancy. Who cares who I really am? In New York, to these people I've encountered, I was Jansen.

And as I stroll into a crowded, cheerful diner called Poppy's, it occurs to me that my time in New York is done. I can do it. I can be Him. At will. And people lap it up.

Soaking wet, I slide into a booth and apologize to the waitress who appears with a glass of water and silverware rolled in a napkin. I explain to her how I've just come from doing a play, and I'd love to give her tickets for tomorrow night's show if she could find it in her heart to bring me a towel.

All smiles, of course she can.

I will have breakfast tonight. I will leave tomorrow morning. I'm glowing inside. You should see me. If you asked me where I'm going next, I would tell you, "Home."

And you'd say "Charlotte, North Carolina?"

And I'd smile and say, "No, friend. LA. I've got this fabulous home in the Hollywood Hills. And the view from my veranda! You should see the Valley at night!"

LA

Chapter 10

Bo ~ the worst wedding in the world ~ as is ~ arrives in LA late and excited ~ sits on the porch and eavesdrops ~ enters his brother's bungalow

The last time my brother Bo and I were together was nine years ago at a wedding in Statesville, North Carolina. He was living in Seattle at the time, and he came down to see one of our cousins get married since we'd all known each other and made a lot of dumb childhood memories. The wedding ceremony and reception was held at a place called Lakewood Park. All it was really was a little pond filled with ducks and surrounded by woods and paved hiking trails. There were playgrounds, too, and a gazebo at one end of the pond that looked as though it might rot apart into the water at any moment.

The wedding was on a Saturday in July, and man it was hot. Since North Carolina was in the midst of a drought, the pond had nearly dried up, so all the ducks were congregated in the largest evaporating puddle of brown water in the center. They were so loud. You could see the lakebed, and it was cracked and the whole place smelled like dead fish. Even worse, since Lakewood was a city park, there were loads of people and their noisy, shitty children in the vicinity, so you had to really strain to hear the preacher.

They were married under one of the four concrete picnic shelters that surrounded the pond. The guests sat at picnic tables. I mean, they tried to decorate the place with flowers and ribbons and such, but it still looked like a bomb shelter.

Afterward, they had their wedding pictures made (you guessed it) under that decrepit gazebo, and my father and his three brothers grilled hamburgers and hotdogs for everyone. A very classy ceremony all around. The bride and groom spent their honeymoon in Myrtle Beach, if that means anything to you.

The only reason I even care to mention it, is because my brother was there.

Though I'm Bo's big brother (by four years), we have one of those relationships where the younger brother feels more like the older brother. What I'm saying is, he's done a lot more with his life than I have with mine. He was married a few years ago, and now has a three-year-old boy. Bo's highly intelligent, too. I don't know what he does for a living, but I'm sure he makes gobs of money. And he's a genuinely nice guy. For instance, listen to what he did at that wedding I was telling you about. During the reception, instead of mingling with our family, he came down to the edge of the dried-up pond where I'd been sitting since the ceremony ended, avoiding people, as my mother would say. He asked me if I wanted to take a walk on the hiking paths, just the two of us. I said all right, and we spent the next hour strolling through the woods of Lakewood Park. I even remember what we talked about. Mostly, we laughed about the Worst Wedding in the World and how funny it was that he'd come all the way from the Pacific Ocean to witness this piece of shit.

Bo never asked me why I still lived with Mom and Dad. He never even told me I should get my own place or anything. And man he hates Mom and Dad.

Instead, he told me all about living in Seattle, and how it rained "every fucking day." Just like I was a regular guy.

If you asked me to tell you when I was happiest, I would probably say it was that afternoon with my little brother. I mean, have you ever been around someone, and you know they just take you as is? That even if they could change you for the better, they wouldn't do it?

It's kind of like that with Bo.

The first thing that passes through my mind when the jet touches down on the runway of LAX is, I'm twenty miles from James Jansen's home. It looks like the tarmac of any other airport from my first class window, but the feel of this city, the sprawl of 10 p.m. light and the mansions and studios and activity they suggest, fills me with energy. As the pilot welcomes us to Los Angeles, local time 10:02 p.m., temp. 81 degrees, I can hardly sit still.

All I can think is *I am home now. I'm home.*

It's after 11:00 when I pay the cab fare and walk through the grass of my brother's lawn toward the front porch. His street is a quiet one. Sprinklers water neighboring yards with a soothing hush. I hear crickets.

There aren't too many trees from what I can tell, and the air smells dry and sharp.

The lights are still on inside his bungalow. Three cars in the driveway. Laughter escapes through the open windows.

I step onto the front porch, and I'll be honest, I'm nervous. Sort of wish I'd let Bo know I was coming. Instead of knocking on the door right away, I set my luggage down on the planked porch and take a seat on the bench.

I pick out four distinct voices coming from a room which I cannot see from the porch. Bo, another man, and two women. I'll bet one of them is his wife. I guess that's what you do on a Friday night when you're married: have friends over who are married, about the same age as you, and sit and laugh in the kitchen over drinks while your child sleeps. Seems a very safe, suburban thing to do.

I eavesdrop on their conversation. It's not terribly interesting. One of the women is talking about how she got stuck in traffic for five hours the other day, and that she was so bored, she sat on the hood of her car and read an entire book. I know that sounds interesting, but the way she tells it is actually pretty dull. You can tell *she* thinks it's a really neat story. I have to stop listening when she says, "And there I am, sitting on the hood of my car at four in the afternoon on the 105, getting a tan and reading a novel!" God, I hope that's his friend's wife.

I wait on his porch for a long time. Finally, after midnight, I stand up since it doesn't seem like those two couples are ever going to say goodnight, and knock on the door. That's one thing I'll say for myself—I'm not a timid knocker.

I hear Bo say, "Who in the world could that be?" and I feel guilty again for not calling him this afternoon.

My heart really thumps as I hear approaching footsteps on the hardwood floor. I stand very tall and straight and remove my sunglasses. The door swings open. Bo and I stand two feet apart, and man do his eyes get wide.

"Lancer!" Oh yeah, he calls me Lancer. I don't know why, but I don't mind. No one else calls me that. No one else really calls me anything. "What are you doing here, man?" he says, but he doesn't say it mean. Just very excited and curious, and I suppose it's a reasonable question to ask someone who's knocked on your door after midnight. He has liquor on his breath and this disappoints me, though I'm not sure why.

I don't say anything, because I don't really know what to say. I just step forward and embrace my brother. He hugs me back, and God it feels good.

"You look great," he tells me. And I do. It's true.

"You, too," I say, but he doesn't really. He's put on some weight. He isn't I-have-to-be-lifted-out-of-my-house-with-a-crane fat. Just, married with one kid fat. Comfortable fat. Suburban fat. We don't look anything alike. I'm definitely much handsomer than Bo. I'm not saying he's ugly or anything. But no one's mistaking him for a movie star.

"Come in," he says, and I lift my two suitcases off the porch and walk inside.

He has a very succinct bungalow that has most certainly benefited from the touch of a woman. Right off, as we walk through the foyer toward the kitchen, I notice these pieces of tribal art. I don't know if they're really tribal, but when I see a stone carving of a guy holding a spear, my first thought is, *Look at that strange tribal art.*

Bo looks so different. He's wearing corduroy pants, leather sandals, and a cream-colored linen shirt that is not tucked in. I guess he's going for the whole I'm-on-a-safari look. I'm Hugo Bossing it of course. He has brown hair like mine, though not as thick and luxurious. Plus, he's only six feet tall and wears glasses. The only glasses I wear are my deep dark shades.

A man and two women are sitting around a kitchen table. There's a candle, a half-empty bottle of Patron, four clear glasses.

"Guys," he says as we enter the small, bright kitchen which smells like scrambled eggs, "Meet my brother, Lance."

Everybody says hi Lance, and I say hi everybody.

Bo's holding my right arm above the elbow, and he starts pointing at people.

"Lance, this is Nick."

"Hi, Nick."

"His wife, Maggie."

"Hi, Maggie."

"Hi, Lance. Wow, has anyone ever told you you look like James Jansen?"

"No, why? Do I?"

"A lot."

Bo says, "And finally, meet Hannah, my wife."

I haven't shaken anybody's hand yet, but I figure I'd better hug my sister-in-law, so I set my suitcases down and she rises and we embrace.

"I wish I could've come to your wedding," I say. And I really do. I just didn't have money to fly out to California four years ago.

"It's so good to meet you, Lance. Bo talks about you all the time."

I sort of doubt that. But I guess you have to say that sort of thing if you're my new sister-in-law. I'm sorry to say she's the avid traffic jam reader. She's very shapely and brown, her hair black.

The downside of my arrival is that I think I break up their little party, because Nick and Maggie stand and say they should probably be getting back to Davie. I really hope Davie's their dog, because anyone who would name a child Davie deserves to die.

I have to pee like you wouldn't believe, so before Bo and Hanna walk their suburban friends out to the car, Bo shows me the way to the bathroom. On the way, he tells me to be quiet because Sam is sleeping. I can't wait to meet Sam. He's my nephew.

Chapter 11

Hannah prepares him a room ~ chats with Bo on the deck ~ sees his sleeping nephew ~ Ani the Anteater ~ breakfast with the Dunkquists ~ recalls their annual trips to N. Myrtle Beach and the hurricane ~ rents a Hummer ~ takes a drive and beholds the Valley

When I emerge from the bathroom, I've washed my face, brushed my teeth, and changed into a pair of plaid pajamas. Hannah has carried my luggage into the guest bedroom at the end of the hall, laid out clean linens, and turned back the comforter. After three nights in that shithole in the Bronx, this room looks cozy and inviting.

I tell Hannah thank you very much for letting me impose on them, and she says it's no trouble at all, but I kind of wonder if she's just being hospitable.

Bo went and married a beautiful woman. She's wearing these Capri pants and a little white tank top with no bra. I know you aren't supposed to notice such attributes on your brother's wife, but man she's got these gazongas like you wouldn't believe.

Hannah tells me again that she's really glad to meet me, which practically assures me that she isn't, and then says it's time for her to turn in.

After she's gone, I unpack my suitcase since I'll probably be staying awhile. I don't feel like going to sleep yet, so I tiptoe out into the hallway and make my way back to the kitchen.

Bo's clearing dishes from the dining room table.

"Want a hand with that?" I ask.

"No, I'll wash them tomorrow."

I sit down at the breakfast table. The glasses of tequila are still there, and I can smell that sweet Mexican liquor.

"You want a drink, Lance?" he asks.

"No thanks."

He clears all of the glasses except one, and fills it about two inches high.

I follow him out the back door.

Their neighborhood truly lies on the outskirts of Altadena. From the small deck, I can see beyond their fenced backyard. The town ends here. No question. Black hills rise in the distance. I wonder what this place will look like in the morning.

We sit down in these highly suburban lawn chairs and Bo takes a sip of tequila.

"It's beautiful here," I say, though I can't really tell. Just seems like the right thing to say at the moment. "And Hannah, she's very sweet."

He touches the back of my head, ruffles my hair.

"Been a long time, hasn't it?" he says.

"Yeah."

"Why are you here, Lance?"

"I quit my job."

"Really? What'd you do?"

"I was a legal assistant. Also, I'd had enough of living in that house with Mom and Dad."

"I can understand that."

"I should've called first, Bo. I'm sorry. I really am."

"You don't ever have to call me, man. You just fuckin' show up. This is your house, too. You all right on money?"

"Yeah, of course." The truth is my treasury has been greatly depleted, down to around $15K.

I look over at him, the crickets chirping, a coyote yapping somewhere in all that darkness. He sips tequila. You ought to see the way he smiles at me.

With some people, I'd feel compelled to tell them the story I've decided upon—how I've come out to LA to stay for awhile. I would want to ask them if it was all right to stay in their house until I found a job, a place to live. Not with Bo. The thing about Bo, which I'm now remembering, is he lives in the moment. He could give a shit about why I'm here. Right now, all that matters to him, is it's a lovely night, and he's sipping tequila, and his brother is beside him. At least I hope he feels this way.

We sit outside for awhile. Sometimes, there's so much to say you can't say any of it. It kind of feels like that tonight. After awhile, Bo struggles to his feet and whispers, "I want to show you something."

I follow him back into the house, and we creep barefooted down the hallway, into a dark room with toys all over the floor.

We stop at the foot of a tiny bed. A darkhaired little boy sleeps with his blanket and a toy robot, thumb in mouth, breathing delicately.

I feel Bo's lips near my ear.

"That's your nephew, Sam," he whispers. "He's three, and I've told him all about you."

I wake with the sun, but I lie in bed for a long time, listening to the movements of Bo's family in the kitchen. Little Sam is awake. I think he's having breakfast because Hannah keeps telling him to finish his oatmeal. But he's more interested in somebody named Ani the Anteater who sounds a lot like Bo and talks in a highly inflective voice about counting, learning the alphabet, and eating ants. Sam has been begging Bo all morning: "Pease do Ani! Again, Daddy! Ani!" Sam knows his letters all the way up to C. I know it's not very impressive, but he's only three. I'm sure he's trying his best.

Since I'm only Lance under this roof, I climb out of bed and don't bother changing into my suit yet. The first thing I do is walk over to the window and open the blinds. I see a swing set, a picnic table, and an inflated aquamarine-colored swimming pool sitting half-full in the blazing morning sun. There are no trees. A couple miles beyond the fence, there are sage-covered hills. It's Saturday. A chorus of lawnmowers already in full voice.

I walk down the hall into the kitchen. Bo is fixing breakfast. I smell eggs and sausage and even grits. We all exchange good mornings and did I sleep okay, and yes, beautifully. Sam is curious and shy of me. I sit down at the breakfast table across from his highchair. He's exceptionally cute, but I guess you have to be cute at three, otherwise, you've got a pretty rough time ahead of you.

Bo sets a cup of black coffee in front of me and a plate of food. We eat together. It's a comfortable meal. Bo and I eat grits. Hannah doesn't. Sam becomes increasingly fussy.

I find out that Bo now designs video games for a living. Hannah is a psychologist, and fuck, I get a little nervous about that. I don't know how you could live with one of those people. All the time, they're studying you, figuring out all the things that are wrong with your brain. I'll have to watch out for her. She's probably already got me pegged. I mean, I don't exactly know the details, but I'm fairly confident I'm fucked up on a whole range of levels. But that's the thing about people—no matter what anyone says, they never think they're crazy. I guess to be really crazy, you can't know that you're crazy. It's kind of funny if you think about it.

We get to talking about our childhood, and you can tell that Hannah is pretty interested to hear what her husband was like as a boy. I tell her that Sam looks just like Bo when he was little, because you know parents love to hear stuff like that.

Then I tell about the vacations we used to take to North Myrtle Beach every August, the week before school started back, how we'd stay in the same motel every year. It was called the Windjamer, and though it wasn't oceanfront, you only had to cross two streets to reach the beach. I can't really tell if it bothers Bo to hear me talk about this stuff. He isn't the biggest fan of Mom and Dad. But just when I think I'm making him uncomfortable, he pipes in about the time we got down there and a hurricane was blowing in. Dad loved hurricanes, and while every other family was getting the hell away from the coast, Dad made us bunker down in our motel room and ride the thing out. I know it sounds pretty exciting and all, but at the time, when all that wind and rain was kicking up, Mom, Bo, and I thought we were going to die.

"I never saw so much wind," Bo says. "Oh, and you remember when Dad walked out into the worst of it and he had to hold onto the rearview mirror so he wouldn't get blown down the street?"

He's smiling at me, and I think we're having one of those moments.

After breakfast, I get Bo to drive me to Exotic Car Rentals of Beverly Hills where I have a reservation for a gleaming yellow Hummer. Actually, I let him drop me at a Starbucks across the street. He shouldn't concern himself with my need for upscale transportation.

Bo tells me he'll pick me up in three hours (he's going to work on a video game he's designing), but I tell him not to worry. I'll catch a cab back to his place.

When he's gone, I buy a hot chocolate and cross Little Santa Monica Boulevard to the rental company and get the luxury Hummer for a week. It comes to $6,295. $895/day. $37/hour. About a penny each second.

You might think that's excessive, but would James Jansen drive anything that had a price tag under $70,000?

I climb behind the wheel of that beautiful machine and take a drive along Mulholland, where I cruise the Santa Monica Mountains. I finally come to one of those overlooks that's featured in practically every movie ever made about dreamful people coming to Hollywood. Usually, the scene occurs at night. We find the characters in a pivotal moment, and all of the Valley lies glittering, beautiful, and unattainable. There'll be a tenor sax playing, or moody synthesizers. The characters will say dramatic things like, "I always wanted this" or "I never should've come to this city." Crying will ensue, and hope will be lost as the lights of LA twinkle indifferently in the backdrop.

But on this bright, hot morning, with midday approaching and dust blowing across the parched ground, it holds none of that passionate, neon magic. I sit on the front bumper of my Hummer, simply registering the environment—haze, distant glimmering chrome, the fly on my hand, the silent crawl of traffic on the highways below, and the blue plate of ocean this will all fall into.

I am alone up here on this spectacular vista, and do you want to know what I'm really thinking? It's not what you'd guess. I'm not full of that anxious hope the aspiring actors come up here to feed. I'm not the least bit dreamy. Not even optimistic. I don't need to hedge myself with optimism, because the things I envision will happen. Dreams are no longer necessary. I'm falling in love with reality.

I own this. All of it. It's my kingdom.

That's what I'm thinking.

Chapter 12

Jansen's star ~ the blonde at the stoplight ~ more shopping ~ watches The Fam having supper ~ talks to Bo in the shower ~ gets dolled up properly ~ waits in line ~ eavesdrops ~ makes a proper Star arrival ~ trouble with the doormen ~ guarantees the termination of their employment

Next, I drive to Hollywood Boulevard and have a stroll down the Walk of Fame. Takes me half an hour, but I finally locate Jansen's star. It has his name on it, and the image of a film camera underneath. As I stand there smiling down at this beautiful tribute, I hear the unmistakable click of cameras.

I look up. A group of Japanese tourists are taking my photograph, and I start to smile for them, but then I realize it's probably not cool, if you're a major celebrity, to get caught standing on top of and smiling down at your very own star.

I depart quickly.

Everyone should own a Hummer for at least one week of their life. It's like driving a tank. I mean the thing barely fits in one lane. And if you relish people noticing when you drive by, choose a flashy color, like yellow.

It's four in the afternoon (I've been driving around all day, familiarizing myself with my town) and I'm sitting at a stoplight on Sunset when this silver Ferrari pulls up beside me. That's the thing about Beverly Hills. Where else in the country is it possible for a Ferrari and a Hummer to pass within twenty miles of each other?

I'm of course sporting my gray Hugo Boss, deep dark shades, and the top is still down, so the wind is blowing through my hair, and the sun is warm on my face. You can't imagine how good I look. The window on the passenger side of the Ferrari hums down and reveals this blonde that I won't even try to describe. But trust me. Not unpleasant to look at.

"I like your tank there, Jim! Is it new?"

"Just got it," I say, and for a second, I worry that perhaps she really knows James Jansen, and therefore, I should appear to know her. But then I realize that the beauty of being a Star is that you don't have to remember anybody. In fact, it enhances the effect if you don't.

"What are you doing tonight?" I ask, because I can.

"La Casa, of course. DJ SuperCas is spinning." I wonder what that means.

The car behind me honks. The light has gone green.

"I may see you there," I say.

She winks, and the Ferrari screeches on through the intersection, the growl of its engine audible for several blocks. I put my banana tank into gear and ease on down Sunset, scanning for the kind of stores where you can drop a few thousand on nice pants.

I'm ready for tonight, but I need things first.

Specifically, cologne, a real watch, a cell phone, and club attire.

By the time I've finished shopping and returned to Altadena, it's seven o'clock. The sun is falling into the Pacific, glazing the hills behind Bo's neighborhood with peachy light. I realize it's pointless to try and hide my Hummer from Bo, so I just park the thing in his driveway.

I walk inside and carry my bags into my bedroom. The Fam is having dinner at the picnic table in the backyard. I watch them while I undress in my room. Bo talks to Sam practically the whole time. So does Hannah. They keep leaning toward their son and making these silly faces. It's neat to watch them when they don't know I'm watching them. This is probably how they act when no one's around. My brother's a good daddy. It sounds funny and strange to say, but I'm proud of him. I really am.

While I'm in the shower, someone knocks on the door, and I hear Bo ask, voice muffled, if he can come in for a minute.

I tell him sure.

He comes in.

"What the fuck is in my driveway?" he says. I'm just standing out of the stream of water, letting the conditioner condition.

"I rented a car."

"That's a Hummer, Lance."

"All they had."

"Isn't that a little expensive?"

"Not as bad as you might think."

"Why do you need a Hummer?"

I can tell you I'm getting pretty tired of these questions.

"Haven't you ever wanted to drive around in something flashy?" I ask.

"Sure. But…Lance, you don't even have a job."

I poke my head out of the shower curtain. "Don't worry about me, Bo. I've got plenty of money."

"You do, huh?" He shakes his head and gives me this smug grin he's always had. "Hungry?" he says.

"Little bit."

"Hannah made Santa Fe rice salad. It's in the fridge if you want some. I wish you'd told me you weren't coming back until this evening. I was kind of hoping we'd all eat outside together."

I guess when you're a family guy like Bo, you really look forward to sitting down to dinner with everyone. It's been five minutes, so I step back under the water and begin rinsing the conditioner from my hair.

"You have plans tonight?" he asks.

"Yeah, I'm going to head back out."

He chuckles, "In the big, bad Hummer," and walks out.

Fuckin' Bo. I love him, but he gets these attitudes sometimes.

The woman at The Closet helped me assemble an outfit of what she called, "extremely chic clubwear." And I've got to tell you, it's like no clothing I've ever owned. I'm wearing a black, silk short-sleeved button-up from Armani. Black leather pants. Armani, as well. And my boots which are alligator or crocodile, cost two grand! I don't even think Partner Jeff would've paid that for footwear.

When I'm dressed, I rub on a little of this new cologne I bought. I'd tell you what it was called, but I can't pronounce it. Sounds very French, and the bottle is green and exceptionally small. $375.00/ounce. It makes me smell like an evergreen forest or something. I don't know. Clarice at Sacs told me it matched my biorhythms.

I get some pomade on my hands and run them through my hair, even apply a little eyeliner (another tip from Clarice). So by the time I'm dolled up properly, I hardly recognize myself. I look very, very hip. You should see me.

The Fam is watching a news program when I pass through the living room. It seems such an adult thing to do—watching the news on a Saturday night. I'd get pretty sad if I really thought about it.

I tell them not to wait up for me, that I might not be back until tomorrow. I can tell that Hannah's kind of blown away that I'm going out on the town and all. I'm guessing that from what Bo's told her, she didn't count me as a terribly happening guy.

I kiss Sam on the forehead on my way out and promise him we'll play in the backyard tomorrow. It's the sort of thing you have to do when you're an uncle.

The nightclub La Casa is in a big warehouse on Hollywood. I let the valet park my Hummer, since that's probably what every good Star would do, slip him a $20 for his trouble (I'm carrying $2,000 in cash in my back pocket) and survey the enormous line. The doors opened at 9 p.m. Three very big, very scary-looking men are standing at the double doors leading into La Casa. A burgundy rope separates them from the crowd of several hundred. They keep pointing at people, unhooking the rope, and letting them inside. When the doors open, I feel the pulse of music vibrate in my chest. Sometimes, they point at someone and shake their head and laugh. These people in turn look highly embarrassed and usually leave immediately.

I've never been to a nightclub. I'm excited and anxious. Everyone looks fabulous. I've never seen so many beautiful people in one place, and this makes me feel kind of small.

I eavesdrop on this pack of girls ahead of me as my section of crowd slowly pushes toward the rope boundary.

"That's him. I kind of know the doorman on our side," this total bombshell directly in front of me says. She smells very good. Delightful even. "He's in my yoga class. He told me to find him and he'd let me in and whoever I brought. You either have to know the doorman, be famous, or look totally fucking hot, otherwise forget it."

"Oh my God, if we get into La Casa, I am totally going to tell everyone I know. I'm going to send out fucking announcements and shit."

"I'm so glad you didn't bring Amanda."

"Are you crazy? No fucking way!"

"I totally agree."

"Yeah, totally."

"Oh totally."

"Whoa, look at the hottie."

"Where?"

I realize that I'm doing this all wrong when I see this white limo pull up. The door opens and this couple steps out who I recognize but can't recall their names. They're Stars for sure. Not the heavyweight I am. Medium Stars.

One of the doormen yells, "Move back!" and the crowd splits.

The couple, extraordinarily dressed, moves quickly through the divided crowd. They pass through the rope barrier as flashbulbs explode everywhere. They're smiling at the doormen, oblivious to the crowd of hopefuls all around them. The doors open for them, and they disappear into the inner dance utopia.

I don't waste one more second standing in this ridiculous line. Instead, I go and find the valet and ask him if he wants to make $200? Sure he does. He follows me into the parking lot, and I tell him to get into the driver's seat, which he does.

"Look, I don't have any X on me, man," he says once we're in.

"I don't want any X. Here," I pull two hundreds from my wallet and hand them over. He's young, early-twenties perhaps, with long, stringy hair. I wonder if he's in a rock band, trying to make it, like everyone else. "Drive me up to the curb and let me out in front of the crowd."

"They won't let you in if they don't know you, man. Doesn't matter how you arrive."

"I'm James Jansen. They'll let me in. Now drive."

He cranks the Hummer and we roll back out onto Hollywood, do a u-turn at the next light, and head back toward La Casa, my heart bumping as we pull up beside the crowd to the front of the line where the white limo stopped just ten minutes ago.

The crowd parts. I take a breath, slip on my shades.

Then I open the door and step out of the Hummer, as nervous as I've ever been in my entire life. I muster this sort of irritated scowl on my face, keep my head slightly down, and walk quickly toward the doormen.

Let me tell you, the eyes are all on me. First, because I stepped out of this huge fucking Hummer like I owned the place, and second, because I think everyone starts to realize who I am.

"James!"

"JJ!"

"I love you, James Jansen!"

I try not to smile, but it's pretty hard when cute women scream that they love you.

But I don't acknowledge them. Sure, if this were a movie premier, I'd stop and sign autographs and wave and blow kisses and be altogether charming as hell. But I'm here to have a good time. I'm taking a chance coming out and mingling with the commoners, so it's imperative that I maintain this nobody-better-fuck-with-me iciness in my face.

I reach the velvet ropeline, and much to my dismay, it has not yet been unhooked.

The three sentinels have turned their collective attention to me.

I remove my sunglasses.

One of the doormen lifts a black notebook off a podium and beings scanning a page of names.

I feel hot in my face.

Cameras are beginning to flash all around me—paparazzi.

"Don't waste your time. I didn't get on the list," I say.

"Well, that's a problem," the doorman with the book says.

I look dead into the eyes of the doorman standing in front of me.

"You know who I am?"

He nods. "Yeah, your last movie was a piece of shit."

"Unhook that motherfucking rope."

This is one tough, jaded fellow, but fear flickers in his eyes when I say this. I guess it's sort of an unwritten rule that you should never piss off powerful people.

The doorman with the book comes over to me, says, "Look, if you aren't in the book—"

"I don't give a shit about your goddamn book. Bill Flanagan, the owner of La Casa, has been a guest in my home for numerous parties. I can't tell you how angry he'd be to find out I've been treated this way."

I have no idea who the owner is. First name that came to mind.

The rope is unhooked, and I'm ushered, apologetically, toward the open door. It sort of scares me, because I don't know what I would've done had that last bit not worked.

I stop in the threshold and turn back to the three doormen.

"Gentlemen," I say. "You will all be fired before the end of the night. I promise you that."

Then I put on my shades and enter the mayhem of La Casa.

Chapter 13

pink purple neon madness ~ DJ SuperCasanova ~ gets a table ~ observes bodyshots ~ surveys the joint and expounds on the philosophy of the hollow generation ~ walks into the center of the dance floor ~ looks up an Asian woman's dress ~ the bachelorette party ~ Kara ~ Richard Haneline ~ gets invited to a premier party ~ slow dances to a fast song

La Casa. Wow. I've never seen anything like this. I'm as over-stimulated as I've ever been—lights flashing, spinning, flickering in pink purple neon. It's all light and motion and sound.

I'm standing just inside the doors taking everything in like I've stepped out of a spacecraft onto a new planet. What strange creatures these are.

A spectacular redhead charges me $30 and stamps the back of my hand and I walk into the crowd. From where I stand, I can see four bars, mirrors behind each one, reflecting the crowd. I count five spinning disco balls.

FAMOUS

On the second level, it's more of the same—a crowd moving together in waves like a field of wheat. More bars. More light. And this constant thumping…boom, boom, boom, boom.

At last, I see the music source. Atop a large column in the center of the dance floor, DJ SuperCasanova stands behind a shelf of keyboards and turntables and ear-shattering speakers. He's this white guy sporting a sequin suit and a sequin top hat, and you can tell he loves his job.

I push my way through the crowd and claim one of the few vacant tables.

I sit there, taking it all in. On the table beside me, a woman has stretched herself out flat on her back and pulled her shirt up over her bra, to expose her bellybutton. One of the men lifts two shotglasses from the table and holds them up.

"Tequila or tequila?" he asks and bursts into laughter.

He straddles the woman, pours a shot very slowly onto her sternum and watches ravenously as the liquor trails into her bellybutton.

"Oh yeah!" the woman cries out. "Suck it! Suck it!"

So he sucks the tequila from her naval and runs his tongue up and down the tats on her stomach, lapping up the liquor and making her belly glisten—much to the delight of their company.

When he finishes, the woman climbs off the table and another girl assumes the position.

More drinking of liquor from orifices ensues, nipples are exposed, and I've got to tell you, it's all fairly entertaining to behold.

111

When I tire of watching the youngfolk beside me, I walk to the nearest bar, order an Absolut, one ice cube, no lime, and return to my table.

I sit there sipping my drink and watching the multitude of dancers. People in LA certainly know how to look good. Nearly all of the men are tall, tan, muscular, possess perfect hair, and have this superficial charisma down cold. For instance, I watch this guy talking to this girl on the outskirts of the dancing mob, and even though I can't hear what they're saying, I can read in his face that the only thing he cares about is the possibility of fucking her brains out a little later. I mean, she's chattering away, and he just keeps nodding and flashing these smiles that aren't really smiles, and looking around every now and then to make sure something more fuckable isn't in the vicinity. Real gentlemen, these LA guys.

And the women. Jeez. Every pair of knockers in the place would win the blue ribbon where I come from. There's just a bunch of beautiful people in this room, and what I'm realizing now is that's what it takes not to be lonely out here. You must have the right clothes, body, hair, smell, accessories, and personality. Oh, but when I say personality, I don't mean you have to be genuinely interesting or original. Personality in the LA sense means you must be able to maintain a conversation which suggests you're worth hooking up with because you possess all of the required embellishments.

I saw a television program once about the whole dilemma of attracting a mate. And there were these pitifully normal-looking people who kept saying things like, "eventually, beauty gets old and people are going to want someone who's actually intelligent and unique and has more to offer than a hard body and nice boobs." I hear those lonely people talking while I watch this crowd of vibrant people, and I'm thinking yeah, hold your breath. People may tolerate friendship with plain, interesting people, but they certainly don't want to fuck them, and believe me, fucking is the end result of all this light and makeup and music and alcohol and drugs and dancing. This is all about finding someone to fuck. It has to be. I mean, the group at the table beside me is only a few millimeters of fabric away from doing it. And the dancing—grinding, rather—is pretty much dry humping. I really feel sorry for those bland people, sitting at home, angry and jilted, waiting for all these beauties to come around and realize how *interesting* they are.

After I finish my drink, I walk into the crowd. I am in no way a dancer. Not even remotely. I reach the center of the dance floor. It's ridiculously loud and hot. People move together all around me—sexually, robotically, gracefully, all uninhibited. There are several columns six or seven feet high, and people dance solo on top of these. I stand at the base of one and look up at this Asian woman who is "lost in the music," as they say. I can see up her dress. She's not a big fan of underwear.

This enormous, beefy black man bumps into me. He holds glow sticks and dances with his eyes closed. Another woman, very tall, is garbed in a wedding dress. She just stands in one place, nothing moving but her head, side to side with the beat.

The disco balls come to life and spit their bursting light all over the walls.

I plow on through the crowd to the other side of the room where a beer bar and more tables line the wall.

I sit down beside a table of five lovely women, and after listening to them gab, I discover they're a bachelorette party. All late twenty-somethings. You can tell they don't come out to places like this very often. I wonder how they got into La Casa anyway. They're all drinking highly colorful drinks garnished with slices of tropical fruit. I imagine that once they're sufficiently liquored up, they'll be stumbling out onto the dance floor with everyone else.

One of them catches me staring.

"Hello." I smile that winning smile.

"Hi."

The other four women now look at me.

"Let me guess," I say, very charmingly, "bachelorette party?"

They smile politely, let out some nervous laughter, and confirm that I'm correct.

"Who's the bride-to-be? No. Let me guess."

I lean back and squint and take them in.

Facing me, they occupy one half of a circular table.

From left to right: (i) a redhead, oldest of the bunch, cute, but the glitter on her cheeks is a little disturbing;

(ii) one of those tiny little blondes that probably have to shop for clothes in the children's department. Short hair and twinkly eyes that shine with something none of her friends possess (hope she's not the bride);

(iii) another blonde, more regular-size, who's athlete-pretty but might be stronger than me (yikes);

(iv) a factory-issue brunette who looks as though she's been smiling since Christmas;

(v) another brunette, who, because of the disinterested way she's staring back at me, I surmise is a lesbian. Quite beautiful though.

I point at the smiley brunette.

"I've got to go with you. You look very bridey."

Incomprehensibly, her smile widens, until I think her face is going to split apart.

"Yep. It's me." They all laugh, and I laugh, too.

"Well, good luck to you and your fiancé. I wish you all the best."

A waitress passes near our tables, and I lift my hand, snag her attention.

"Another round for the ladies please, and an Absolut for me, one ice cube, no lime."

"Certainly."

The ladies all thank me and make excuses about how they'd better not drink too much since their partying days are long since gone. But boy when their fruity drinks are replenished, and I've suavely toasted the bride-to-be, they suck them down like you wouldn't believe.

The glittery redhead suddenly lights up and exclaims how rude we all are because we don't even know each other's names.

"This is…" She proceeds to name all five women in about three nanoseconds. I'm awful with names, so the only one I remember is the marvelous blonde. Kara.

"I'm Jim," I say and I reach across and shake everyone's hand very delicately.

The lesbian cocks her head.

"What's your last name?" she asks.

I can't tell you how happy that makes me, but I play it very cool. Hesitating. Like I don't want to say.

"Jansen," I say, extremely understated-like.

The athletic blonde says, *"Down From the Sleeping Trees* Jansen?" Her eyes are about to pop out of her head. I'm serious.

But I just nod and look away like they're making me feel uncomfortable. They're not, incidentally. I'm loving every minute of it.

One of them says holy shit. I hear more nervous giggling.

I kind of don't know what to say to them now. I mean, unless they start asking me questions, I've got nothing.

When I turn back to face them, you wouldn't believe the shock on their faces. All except for Kara. She's just staring at me with her calm, sweet eyes.

A hand squeezes my shoulder.

"Jim?"

Richard Haneline is standing above me. He's a Star. A medium Star. Very recognizable. He isn't handsome in the Hollywood sense. Just distinctive-looking. A long, pointy nose and piercing eyes. He always stars in these Vietnam flicks, playing the renegade solider or the bad guy. Some people just look like the bad guy, I guess. He's always blowing shit up and going off the deep end.

I stand up and smile and shake his hand, wondering if I call him Rich or Richard or some nickname. I didn't even know I knew the guy.

"Great to see you out, Jim. You get my message?"

"No, my voicemail's been fucked up."

I'm taller than Richard Haneline and much better-looking. I focus on these little things to keep from fainting.

"Look, I'm having a party next Tuesday after the premiere. Feel up to coming?"

"Absolutely."

A woman calls out "Rich!" from the dance floor.

He waves to this perfect brunette.

"Jim, if I don't see you again tonight, I'll call you." He starts to walk back onto the dance floor.

I grab his arm. "My phone's going to be out of commission for a few days. Here." I take a cash receipt, tear off a section, and scribble my new cell number down. "Use this number. Just call me tomorrow or Monday with details."

"Sounds good. Hey, guy, I'm so happy to finally see you out. I think it's terrific."

He seems to want to say more, but instead he slaps my shoulder and backpedals into the tangle of dancers.

When I turn around, I see that the five ladies of bachelorette party fame have not moved. To tell you the truth, I think they're fairly star-struck. And between seeing me and Haneline, that's understandable.

I go ahead and take a seat across from them. The blonde and I lock eyes.

"You dance?" I ask her. She shrugs—very cute. I think she's adorable. Perhaps it's mean of me not to ask the bride-to-be to dance, but I can't bring myself to do it. I don't want to dance with anyone except this little blonde.

"I'm a terrible dancer," I say.

"Me, too."

"Then shall we?"

Kara polishes off her fruity drink and rises from her chair. I'm praying for a slow song, but something tells me they don't ever play slow songs in this place.

I take her by the hand and lead her out onto the dance floor. Her hand is very small and warm. Would it kill DJ SuperCasanova to play a slow song?

Kara only comes up to my shoulder. When we find a spot in the crowd, I lean down and put my lips to her left ear. The beat pulses on relentlessly. Boom…Boom…Boom…Boom.

"Would you mind if we slow-danced to this?" I ask.

I hope I haven't hurt her eardrum, but I have to scream to be heard.

She looks up at me, smiles, shakes her head.

I cup the small of her back and pull her body into mine. She's wearing a sleeveless black dress and she smells like someone I could love. I know that sounds strange. But right now, I don't give the first shit about anything except standing here with her, moving together at our own pace. Even though we haven't said three words to each other, I know her more than anyone I've met since leaving North Carolina, and underneath all this noise, I'll bet we hear the same song.

Chapter 14

leaves La Casa ~ takes Kara home ~ prepares his specialty for the Dunkquists ~ talks with Bo about marriage and Hannah ~ plays with Sam in the swimming pool

We slow dance through two more fast songs, and it feels so good being pressed up against her. Finally she pulls my ear down to her mouth and tells me that the music is hurting her ears. It's hurting mine, too. I ask her if she wants to leave, because it kind of seems that way. She does. I'm ready to go, too. Even though I haven't been here very long, I've seen all I care to see of LA club life. And of course, I secured an invite to my good pal, Richard Haneline's, movie premiere and party.

On a side note, his most recent movie was called *The Soldier*. It's about a solider who has to sneak behind enemy lines in World War I to kill some general or colonel. And the movie is actually pretty decent, but do you think they could've put a tad more thought into the title? I just hate stuff like that.

I hold Kara's hand again and lead her out of the crowd. We return to the table of her four dance-shy friends and she tells them she isn't feeling well, and that I've offered to take her home. Of course, her friends are very concerned about her, but I also catch a whiff of envy.

You think you'd enter and exit through the same doors, but actually you exit out the side of the building. I guess those three fuckheads at the door wouldn't want any of the La Casa hopefuls to know that anyone ever leaves the place.

Kara and I stand in the warm evening while the long-haired valet goes searching for my car. You can still feel the throbbing music, but it's muffled enough to hear the traffic cruising up and down Hollywood and the murmur of the crowd standing in line just around the corner of the building.

"Thank you," Kara says as I hear my Hummer crank somewhere out in the parking lot darkness. "I just had to get out of there."

The Hummer pulls up to the curb, and I usher Kara to the passenger side, open the door for her, and help her in. I know it sounds mean, but I don't tip the valet. I mean the guy's made $200 off me already tonight. I think that's sufficient. Even still, he sighs and rolls his eyes when I get in without tipping him.

So I head back out onto Hollywood and we just drive for awhile in the direction of UCLA.

Kara's quiet. I can't tell if something's wrong since I don't really know her, but I can't believe she isn't more excited to be riding in James Jansen's Hummer.

"Everything all right?" I ask.

"I'm a little nervous," she says.

"Why?" I know why, but I'd love to hear her say it.

"I'm just a little in awe. I don't really know how to act. My friends would be talking your ear off, but I'm…I don't know."

"I don't want you to be uncomfortable," I say, and it's true. I really don't. I want her to be comfortably in awe.

"Turn here," she says.

"How about this?" I say. "Pretend I'm just some guy you met in the club."

"I wouldn't have met any guys in that club. They certainly wouldn't be driving me home. I don't know if you noticed, but everyone in that place is swimming in the kiddie pool."

"Huh?"

"Sorry, bad analogy. They're shallow."

"Oh. Yes, I agree."

"Look, Jim?"

"Yeah?"

"I don't know how this normally works for you. I'm sure you get women like crazy, but I'm not one of those. Okay?"

"Okay."

"I really…I'm incapable of bullshit. That's who I am. So I'm going to just say it. The reason you're taking me home, the reason I wanted you to, beyond the fact that I despise clubs, is we made a connection. It has nothing to do with who you are, your fame I mean. I honestly felt something that has nothing to do with any of that. And I know that I'm not supposed to be telling you this. Maybe you'd rather we…turn here…maybe you'd rather we played a little game where neither of us admits how incredible that was on the dance floor, but that's not me. I'm sorry if I'm ruining this for you."

"It was," I say.

"What?"

"It was incredible dancing with you, Kara."

She smiles and brushes her hair behind her ears.

"That's my building up ahead."

I turn into the parking lot of a four-story apartment building on the outskirts of the UCLA campus. I kind of wonder if she's going to invite me up. This sounds strange, but part of me hopes she doesn't.

"I'll kill the suspense for you. I'm not going to ask you up," she says as I pull up to the main entrance. "I'm sorry." She unbuckles her seatbelt but doesn't open the door yet.

"This is it?" For some reason, the possibility of her getting out of this car and me not ever seeing her again turns me desperate. "Could I call you?"

"What are you doing tomorrow?" she says, opening the door and stepping out.

"No plans."

"Pick me up at eleven if you want to. Right here. I'll spend the day with you."

"I don't even know your—"

"You will. For now, just enjoy what happened tonight. Relish it. It was pure."

She slams the door and I wait until she's inside the building before driving away. I'm tempted to hit another club or bar, or just cruise through the mansions in the hills.

But instead, I decide to head on home and relish it.

I rise at 6:30 before anyone else and creep into the kitchen and start assembling the ingredients for the only dish I know how to make—a Mexican omelet.

Since there's four of us, I break a dozen eggs into a glass mixing bowl. Then I shred half a block of sharp cheddar and what's left of a block of monetary jack. Then I cut up some tomatoes, add a third of a cup of hot chipotle salsa, sauté some onion, green pepper, and a heap of diced jalapeno peppers. I add everything to the eggs, throw in salt and pepper and red pepper and a tablespoon of Tabasco sauce. Then I whisk it all together and dump the whole runny mixture into a buttered frying pan.

The Dunkquists start drifting into the kitchen as the smell of my Mexican omelet fills the house. I've gone ahead and brewed a pot of coffee so strong it could run a car engine, and I'm sitting on the kitchen counter, staring out the window at those hills catching early morning sun.

"You didn't have to do this, Lance," Hannah says as she opens a cabinet and retrieves her Lakers coffee mug. She pours herself a cup, sips it, winces. Without saying a word, she dumps it into the sink, and takes a teabag from a glass jar. As she fills a saucepan with water and fires up the gas on the stove, Bo enters in underwear and a tee-shirt.

"That looks interesting," she says, staring down into the congealing eggs.

"Surprised to see you up so early," Bo says to me. "Smells great."

He takes a mug from the cabinet bearing the logo of his software company (the talons of a hawk in swift descent) and fills it with my unwanted coffee. He sips it, looks at me, and smiles.

"Now that's what coffee's supposed to taste like."

"You tasted this yet, Hannah?"

"Little strong for me," she says flatly, coldly. I am unfortunately coming to the realization that my brother married a real fucking bitch.

"Where'd you go last night?" Bo asks, leaning against the counter beside me. I'm wearing a red and blue Ralph Lauren robe, incidentally. Very classy.

"This dance club."

"Oh? I didn't think you liked that sort of thing."

"I don't, but I was curious to see some LA nightlife."

"Meet anybody?"

"I did actually. I'm going to spend the day with her."

I notice that Hannah is staring at me like she wants to ask me something. She might loath me.

"Could you stir the eggs, Hannah?" I ask as nicely as I possibly can.

She takes the wooden spatula, turns her back to us, and stirs the eggs.

"So are you going to look for a job next week, Lance?" she asks.

"I sure am."

"And you were a legal assistant up until a week ago?"

"Yes." I sip my coffee. I hate being asked questions by people who dislike me.

"What kind of work do you have in mind?"

"Whatever's available. Doesn't really matter, long as it pays decent."

Little feet come slapping down the hall, and Sam runs into the kitchen. He stops suddenly when he sees me. You can tell that he forgot I was here. He just sort of looks at me for a moment, not unlike the way his mother does. But then he smiles and runs over to Bo and hangs on his leg.

"I wanna swim," he says, looking up into his daddy's eyes.

"Gotta eat first, pal."

"Swim!"

"Aren't you hungry?"

Sam considers this, then nods.

"As soon as you eat, you can go swim. I'll bet Lance would love to swim with you. You remember Uncle Lance?"

"No, just you."

"Okay, okay." Bo winks at me. "Let's get in your highchair. Uncle Lance made breakfast for everyone."

After breakfast, I offer to wash the dishes, but Hannah won't let me. She didn't touch the omelet I made, even though it was very tasty.

Since it's just past nine, the brutal heat has not set in. Bo and I put on swimming trunks, and Sam leads us out into the backyard. The water in the swimming pool is tepid and grass clippings float on the surface. We turn the pool upside down. This is unbearable to Sam, who starts sobbing and screaming because I guess he thinks that was the only water around. He settles down once Bo unwinds the garden hose and starts refilling the pool.

Sam loves water. He climbs into the pool while it's filling and just sits there on the plastic, watching the stream of water flowing out of the nozzle.

Bo and I sit on the picnic table. It feels exceptionally pleasant out here at this hour of the morning. I take off my shirt.

Once the pool is filled, Bo takes the hose away from Sam and cuts off the water. Apparently, Sam enjoys squirting adults who don't care to get wet.

"So tell me about being married," I say, since neither of us have yet said a word and I'm a bit curious anyway.

Bo smiles and removes his shirt. I'm in exceedingly better physical condition than my brother.

"It's good," he says. "It really is."

I don't believe him of course.

"Really?"

"Yeah."

"Would you tell me if it wasn't?"

"I don't know."

"Hannah's great."

"Yep."

"Why doesn't she like me?"

He looks at me.

"What are you talking about?"

"I know when someone doesn't like me. She doesn't."

He sighs.

"I think the whole just showing up unannounced thing kind of got to her, you know?"

I don't know. If I were married and my spouse's brother showed up without calling, I'd be thrilled to take them in and give them a bed and food, because that's what you do for family.

"I'll apologize," I say, and Bo doesn't say anything, and this really upsets me, because he should tell me I don't have to apologize for anything to his wife, since I'm his brother after all. *You just fuckin' show up. This is your house, too.* Didn't he say that to me the night I came here?

Hannah steps out onto the back porch and asks if she can speak to Bo for a minute. The way Bo doesn't say anything, but just hops off the table and jogs back toward the house confirms two things for me:

(i) he's scared shitless of that woman; and

(ii) he hates her exponentially more than I do.

Sam is pretty engrossed with playing in the pool when Bo runs back into the house, but he notices. I guess kids always notice when their parents leave. Sam immediately looks at me like "should I be upset about this?" and I'm thinking please don't start crying, but I guess he feels comfortable with me because he returns his attention to the water toys.

I step down into the grass and walk over to the pool. "Hey, there, Sam."

He looks up at me but doesn't say anything. I step into the pool. The water is cool.

"Can I sit down, Sam?"

He looks at me but still won't talk. I sit down and shiver as the cool water comes up to my bellybutton. Sam is playing with a green, plastic boat. He's sailing it through the water. After awhile, he hands me a red boat. I sail it through the water just like he's doing. He takes the red boat back and gives me the green one.

"Sam?" He looks up at me, squinting now as the sun has come up over those distant hills. "I'm your uncle. Uncle Lance. I love you, Sam."

He looks down into the blue water. I think he's more interested in the boat.

Chapter 15

on the road with Kara ~ stops for snacks ~ what to call him ~ Los Padres ~ have their picture made at an overlook ~ hikes up Mt. Pinos ~ picnics in the meadow ~ why Kara's dead to art ~ takes a nap ~ wakes and kisses her ~ a phone call from Rich

I arrive at Kara's apartment building at 10:59. It's a glorious Sunday morning, and she's glorious in it.

She climbs into the Hummer. I ask her where she wants to go, and she tells me to surprise her. She's wearing these little khaki hiking shorts, a navy tank top, and deep dark shades like mine. Her skin smells like coconut and it glistens.

California is full of wonders: Yosemite, Kings Canyon, Sequoia, Redwood, Death Valley, Lassen Volcanic, the Channel Islands…but these paradises are all so far away, so Bo suggested I take Kara north up I-5 into Los Padres National Forest.

At high speed, a Hummer is pretty loud. Especially on the interstate, with the top down and a steady sixty-mile an hour wind pummeling your face. But I don't mind, and I'll tell you why. It forces a comfortable silence. If Kara and I were in my brother's minivan, it would be quiet, and there would be this pressure to make engaging conversation. I don't think I've ever been on the business end of an engaging conversation in my life.

But things are going very well. I glance over every now and then, and Kara's leaning back in the seat, just taking it all in. She seems to be highly relaxed, and sometimes when she sees me look at her, she smiles and pats my hand, the way a wife might do. You should see it.

In Castaic, I get off the interstate and pull into the parking lot of a convenience store. There's an ice-filled cooler in the back seat which I swiped from Bo's garage. I point it out to Kara and tell her we should go in, pick out drinks and food for lunch.

We walk through the gravely parking lot. The sun is bright and hot.

Inside the store, it's cool and smoky.

I pick out two pimento cheese sandwiches from the freezer and a six-pack of soda. At the register, I wait for Kara. The clerk is an old man. He smokes an unfiltered cigarette and just stares at me, like he knows who I am and could give a shit. You've got to respect that.

Kara sets a tuna sandwich and a pint of vanilla ice cream on the counter and I pay for everything with warm, soft cash.

We walk back out into the noonday heat and stow everything in the cooler.

As I put the key into the ignition, Kara touches my arm.

"Jim, I have to tell you, I'm having a tough time getting past the whole celebrity thing."

"Really?"

"Yeah, I was doing fine until this morning. But all my friends from last night's party called, and it's not their fault, but they were just making such a huge deal out of our date today. I wish I didn't even know who you were. Do you know what I mean? I'm just afraid it's coloring this experience for me."

"You think about things a lot, don't you?"

She smiles and touches my arm again. "Often to my own detriment." I love it when she touches my arm.

"I've just had maybe the best idea ever," I say, and it's true. I have a terrific one.

"What?"

"I'm not Jim Jansen."

"Huh?"

"I'm not Jim Jansen anymore."

"Well, who are you?"

"Call me Lance."

"Lance?" She giggles. "Why?"

"I'm serious."

"I'm not going to call you Lance."

"What's wrong with Lance?"

"It's not your name."

"Pretend it is."

"This is too weird."

"Weirder than spending a day with the James Jansen?"

She tilts her head in thought, and I glimpse myself in the reflection of her sunglasses: khaki pants, white shirt with the sleeves rolled up. I've borrowed my brother's leather sandals. I smile at my reflection and Kara thinks I've smiled at her.

"What?" she says.

"So what's my name?"

"Lance, I guess."

"You don't like it?"

"You just don't look like a Lance. What's your last name going to be?"

"Dunkquist."

She guffaws. "Lance Dunkquist?"

"Lance Blue Dunkquist."

She punches my arm very flirtatiously and laughs.

"I know it's a stupid name," I say.

"Well, start the car, Lance Blue Dunkquist, and let's get to wherever we're going."

Interstate 5 climbs above four thousand feet and the air turns cooler.

At Tejon Pass, we pull onto the shoulder and have our picture taken by an elderly couple on a Sunday drive up from Santa Barbara. I introduce myself as Lance. They are sweet old folks. The kind that make the prospect of old age not quite so horrifying. When we're back in the Hummer and driving along the winding, secondary road, I tell Kara how seeing an old couple like that makes me look forward to getting older, and she looks at me like I've uttered a great truth or something. She holds my hand. I think we're having one of those moments, and I guess the point of life is having as many of them as you can. This is my second. It feels even better than the first.

We park at the end of a national forest road at the foot of Mt. Pinos. It's a few minutes past one. Most of the picnic tables are occupied by families. They're a beautiful thing when you're with someone like Kara. If I were alone and feeling like myself, I would hate them.

Since the cooler is small and equipped with a shoulder strap, I lift it from the back seat and ask Kara to carry the blanket.

We set out up a hiking trail that meanders through the conifers.

Clouds obscure the sun.

The air turns even cooler.

No one's on the trail.

We walk side by side.

The path climbs and climbs.

After an hour, we reach a meadow strewn with boulders and patches of old snow near the summit. Kara says that this would be a lovely spot to stop, and I agree. We're both a little winded, a little sweaty.

I follow Kara off the trail, and she finds a level plane of grass and spreads the blanket. We remove our footwear and stroll barefooted through the warm grass. Then we sit down on the blanket, and I open the cooler. Plunging my hand into the ice, I emerge with two cans of cola and our sandwiches. The high altitude has created pressure inside the bag of potato chips.

We're hungry from the hike, and we eat in silence. The sandwich tastes good. I love pimento cheese, even though I'm not exactly sure what it is.

I'm so happy. If you knew me at all, you could tell.

We pass the pint of ice cream back and forth. It's soft and cold and gone in no time.

I stretch out on the blanket and put on my shades because the sun is directly overhead. Kara wipes her mouth on her navy tank top (I forgot to bring napkins) and then she crawls over to me and cuddles up with her head on my shoulder, her hand on my chest.

Says, "This is so nice. Not at all what I thought today would be like."

"What'd you expect?"

"I was afraid you would try to blow my mind. I sort of thought we'd be flying up to San Francisco or down to Mexico. This is so…understated. You couldn't have planned it any better."

"You know a lot about me, but I don't even know one thing about you," I tell her as I begin running my fingers through her hair. "Except where you live and that one of your friends is getting married soon."

"I'm a grad student," she says. She stretches one of her legs over mine. "I'm in the art history program at UCLA. Which means I'll be teaching the rest of my life."

"What's your favorite painting?"

"I don't have one. I can't enjoy them anymore. All I see is technique. Color. Brushstrokes. I see the artist. His life. What else was happening in the world while he created the work. I see what everyone else has written about it. I see other paintings that knock him off. That he knocks off. I see everything but the work itself. By the time I've finished my dissertation, I'll know everything about renaissance period work, except how to be moved by it."

"What was your favorite painting when you could still feel?"

She sits up on one elbow. Our faces are inches apart. She has very pink, perfect lips. "I don't remember. But I'm sure someone ruined it for me." She smiles and takes off my sunglasses.

We keep talking. About small things mostly. She doesn't ask me anything about being famous, and this is a relief, because I wouldn't feel much up to discussing it. She tells me about her roommate, Colleen, and the cat named Slick who inhabits their apartment (in violation of the lease). While she's talking, I try thinking of what I might tell her about my life. I can't really come up with anything, so I just keep asking her questions.

After awhile, she puts her head back on my shoulder.

The breeze is constant.

We close our eyes and sleep.

I wake before Kara. The only sound is wind rustling the grass blades. I stare at her face. The mountains. The pines. Bakersfield to the north and the trace of the San Andreas Fault, cutting through these hills. To the west, far, far beyond, the sky blue meets a deeper blue, and I wonder, *Is that the sea?*

I look back into Kara's face. I kiss her forehead, her left cheek, right cheek. Her eyes open. We kiss open-mouthed for a long time.

As evening rolls in from the east, we drive down out of the hills into warmer air. LA looks beautiful in the distance. Lights winking on in the evening haze. It's not such an indifferent place if you know what you're doing.

I'm feeling so good. It's like I don't even care what happens now, because I've had this day with Kara. She's so liberating. I glance at her sitting in the passenger seat. She's called me Lance ever since we had our discussion in the convenience store parking lot, and the name isn't so bad coming off her lips.

"Can I see your place?" she asks, jolting me out of my thoughts.

"Really?"

"I want to see where you live, Jim. I think I'm ready for it."

I don't say anything.

"Is that all right?" she asks.

My cell rings. First call on the new phone. I fish it out of my pocket.

"Hello?"

"Jim! Rich!"

"Rich, what's up?"

"I didn't see you again at La Casa, so I thought I'd call about Tuesday night. The premiere's at the El Capitan. How many people you bringing?"

"Just me and a date."

"I'll have my assistant add you to the guest list. The party should be a real kick. Brendan's coming. Max and Brody, too. Everyone'll be just thrilled to see you. It's going to be lavish."

"Sounds good."

"Okay, then. You need anything, anything at all, I'm your man."

"You're a good friend, Rich."

"Where are you? Sounds like you're in a plane or something."

"Actually, I'm heading down the 405. I spent the day with this lovely woman I met last night at the club." I look at Kara as I say this. Homerun.

"You must have the top down on your Porsche."

"Oh yeah. I guess you can hear all the wind."

"Well, you're breaking up. I'll see you Tuesday then. What's that?" he says to someone else. "Oh yes, Margot sends her love."

"Right back at her."

"He says right back at you, babe."

"What? Oh, that hurts. She asks if your torrid love affair is back on."

"Absolutely."

"Well then, goodnight, you bastard."

I close the phone and look over at Kara.

"Do you have plans Tuesday evening?"

"Nothing in stone."

"Would you come with me to a movie premier and a party afterward?"

Her eyes kindle, then die.

"Jim, I'd be terrible company."

"No you wouldn't."

"It's no fun being the only nobody at a party."

"You aren't a nobody."

"No offense, but in a roomful of stars, I'm a nobody. You don't want to take me, Jim."

"I do. And I don't want to hear you say that nobody business anymore."

"You don't have any idea what it's like to be obscure. And the prospect of having to mingle with movie stars isn't enjoyable for me."

"If you want to have a relationship with me, Kara, it's something you'll have to learn to deal with. People respect me. They'll respect my date."

She sighs. You can tell that deep down she really wants to go. I mean, who wouldn't?

"You better hold my hand through the whole thing. I mean it, Jim."

"What happened to Lance?"

She doesn't ask to see my house again. I drop Kara at her apartment and promise to call her tomorrow with details of the premiere. It's devastating watching her walk away toward the lobby of her building.

The best day of my life has ended.

Chapter 16

back in time for dinner ~ takes a stroll with Bo and cold beer ~ talks about Kara ~ sits on a bleacher and talks about fame ~ insomnia, then sleep

The Dunkquists are just sitting down to dinner when I return to Altadena. Hannah has prepared something called white chili and jalapeno cornbread. She tells me she's glad I got back in time to join them.

After dinner, I ask Bo to take a walk with me, and he grabs a couple bottles of German beer from the fridge and checks with Hannah to see if it'd be all right for him to step out for a minute. I think it's pretty sad when an adult has to ask permission to go outside.

"Your son needs a bath," she says from the kitchen sink. We're standing in the foyer by the front door.

"I'll give him one when I get back."

"It's seven forty-five, Bo."

"Then you wash him, Hannah, and I'll do the dishes."

Hannah drops a drinking glass into the dishwater (it breaks) and walks over to the breakfast table where Sam still sits in his highchair, playing with his food. As she slides out the tray, Bo pushes open the front door, and I follow him outside.

I love Bo's neighborhood at night. The crickets are chirping, the bungalows all aglow. The street is empty so we walk right down the middle of it, the lawn sprinklers whispering on either side of us, the soles of our loafers dragging along the pavement. Bo hands me a beer and a bottle opener from his pocket.

"Sorry I got you in trouble back there," I say.

"Not your fault, Lance. We, uh…we have some things to work on. Hannah's an intense person." I'm not really sure, but I think that just means spoiled bitch.

The beer is dark, thick-tasting, and creamy, like cold, black coffee. I like it.

I tell Bo about my day with Kara. About Mt. Pinos and the meadow. I describe what she looks like, how she's a grad student at UCLA. He's so happy for me. You know how sometimes, when you tell someone a piece of good news about yourself, you can tell they don't really care? It's not like that at all with Bo. It's like *he'd* spent the day with Kara.

We walk all the way to this soccer field. I feel lightheaded in a pleasant way. I think it's from this good, strong beer. The goals are rusted, nets tattered. Bo and I head for the solitary bleacher. The sound of its metal resonating under our feet reminds me of playing baseball in middle school. That was the last good time before now.

We sit looking out across the playing field and drinking beer.

"Lance," Bo says, "I'm glad you're here, pal. I really am."

I look at my brother and smile. I think I'll just ask him.

"Could I have your opinion on something?" I say.

"Sure."

I polish off the rest of my beer and set the bottle beside me.

"I haven't really told Kara the truth about some things."

"Like what?"

"About living with Mom and Dad for seventeen years and being sort of a loser."

"You aren't a loser, Lance."

"Oh, I know."

"Lance." He takes hold of my arm and finds my eyes. "You aren't a loser. I've always thought you had this special insight, that you really saw people for what they were."

"Who'd you want to be when you were a kid?"

"You mean like a profession?"

"No, a person. Like a star."

"Oh." He considers this for a moment. "When I was thirteen, I wanted to be Tommy Fields."

"From The No-Names?"

"Yeah."

I laugh, because Tommy Fields was a skinny, long-haired rock star from the mid-70's. He was always being rebellious in interviews, and all of the songs he wrote were titled "Bad Love" or "Dying for You." Real subtle themes. But he accidentally lit himself on fire during a concert in 1980, and no one ever heard about him after that.

"Why'd you want to be him?" I ask.

"I don't know. It was just a stupid fantasy."

"No, really. Think about it."

He thinks about it.

"Well, I loved rock-and-roll. I mean, who doesn't want to stand in front of a screaming crowd? It'd be a thrill."

"Yeah. To have everyone know you and love you. Doesn't it ever make you sad being obscure?"

"I don't understand."

"Right now, you and I are sitting here in a huge, exciting world, just two normal guys that no one's ever heard of, and no one ever will. Doesn't that make you sad?"

"No."

"Well, it does me."

"Why?"

"Because when I die, I'll be instantly forgotten. You and Mom and Dad will remember me, but that's just until you croak. Think about how presidents feel, even the bad ones. And movie stars. Even washed-up ones. They know that even if they were to die tomorrow, they'd be remembered. They made a dent, you know? Can you imagine what that must feel like?"

"Probably not as good as you think, Lance."

"No. Better. I think it must be the best feeling in the world."

Bo finishes his beer and slings the bottle out into the grass.

"You want to know what the best feeling in the world is?" he asks me. "Happens to me once a day. It's ten-thirty, the news has ended. I turn off the television, and before I go to bed, I walk down the hallway and crack the door to Sam's room. And I peek in at my son, sleeping peacefully in bed, under a roof I've provided for him. That, Lance, is the best feeling in the world."

I get up from the bleacher and recover Bo's empty bottle from the grass. I don't condone littering. When I return, I see that Bo has stretched himself out on the top rung, staring up at the hazy stars.

"That's just an instinctive feeling," I say to him, a little angry. "And anyone with a functioning reproductive system can have it."

"You're losing me, pal. I think you're confused. And that's fine. Nothing wrong with that. Maybe you could go talk to someone like Hannah, and they could help you figure out what you want."

"I know what I want."

Bo sits up and looks at me.

"What do you want?" he asks me.

Of course I don't tell him.

Instead, I start off down the street.

It's after one o'clock in the morning. The house is so quiet. I can only hear the refrigerator cutting on and off, and outside, the chirp of crickets.

I sit in a rocking chair by the window. Light from a telephone pole in the backyard floods between the blinds and spreads a pattern of lucent rectangles across my chest, and on the hardwood floor.

I am very awake. Fearfully awake. In two days I have a movie premier and a party to attend. Other social engagements will surely follow. It's tempting to carry on as I have this past week. No, not tempting. Safe. I could find a job, hit the clubs on weekends, get recognized occasionally, play at being Him.

But that's all I've done, and all I would be doing. Playing. I realize this now. And perhaps playing would be satisfactory for most people, but it isn't good enough for me any longer. Every time I come back to this house as Lance, the pain intensifies. I was not meant to be this man. I was not meant to be obscure.

I hold a scrap of paper which I've carried around in my wallet for two years, reading it over and over in the eerie, orange light.

James Jansen
203 Carmella Drive
Beverly Hills, California. 90213.

It's the address of my new home. It makes me smile to think of it, and a peace settles upon me.

I can sleep now.

Chapter 17

Bo Bo's ~ the namedropper ~ the Jansen bungalow ~ breakfast in the Hummer ~ a brief synopsis of Jansen's public profile during the last year ~ Until the End of Time: a screenplay ~ follows the white Porsche ~ makes the namedropper's day ~ Universal Studios ~ the gated life

I wake before dawn, slip into this pinstripe Brooks Brothers shirt and khaki slacks, and tiptoe out of the house. There's a diner called Bo Bo's on Sunset which looks to be the only thing open at this hour of the morning, so I stop off and order a cup of coffee and a bearclaw.

There are these people sitting in one of the booths still wearing their evening attire from the previous night, and you can tell they're trying to act very excited about being in a diner after partying all night, but they look dead tired. While the cashier withdraws my bearclaw from the pastry case, I overhear this one guy who's completely monopolizing the conversation, busily listing all the Stars he saw.

"…Brad Locket. Tony Vincent. Angela *Murphy*. I got a drink for her. A bone dry martini, 'cause I read somewhere that was her favorite. And you know what she said to me? 'I was just thinking how I could use one of these. How thoughtful.' She was already sloshed I think. I told her about my screenplay, and she said she'd love to read it. You fuckin' believe that? I'm going to drop it off at her agent's office this afternoon. You know, this is how careers get started."

You really wouldn't believe what happens next. The namedropper stops mid-sentence, and I hear him whisper, "Look who's standing at the counter." Any other time, I'd be mightily pleased to have this recognition, but today is an important day for me, and I can't tolerate the distractions of faking fame.

I haven't turned around yet, but I hear the young man slide out of the booth and begin walking across the diner toward me. The cashier hands me the bearclaw and changes my five dollar bill. I gather up my pastry and steaming cup of coffee, and when I turn around, this eager young face stands before me, nervous and hopeful. He sports—well, sports is too strong a word— he's attempting to wear a tux, but it's about half a size too large for him. It looks as though he borrowed it off his big brother.

"Mr. Jansen," he says, and then freezes.

"Yes?" I ask impatiently.

He closes his eyes, takes a big breath. I walk on toward the door, but he steps in front of me.

"Please, I know you're very busy, but please just let me say this." He swallows and meets my gaze. "You're my favorite actor in the entire world, and I've written a screenplay with you in mind for the lead. Can I give this to you? Would you take it and not throw it away?" From under his arm, he pulls out this script and practically shoves the thing in my face.

"You know," I say, accepting the script and smiling, "I'm actually looking for my next project right now. What's your name?" He has to think about this for a moment.

"M. Connor Bennett."

"Well, Connor. Tell you what. I'm going to read this today, and if I like it, we'll be in touch."

"Oh my God. Thank you so much, Mr. Jansen. Thank you. Thank you. Thank you. My contact info is on the cover page. Holy shit."

Then he hugs me.

I drive up into the Hollywood Hills.

It takes me an hour to find Carmella Drive, this little road off Laurel Canyon.

At seven in the morning, it's quiet and beautiful. You can't really see the houses from the road, since most of them are enclosed by stone walls, but every so often, you'll catch a peek through a gate or a thin spot in the foliage. It makes my head swim to think that a Star or director or producer lives in every house I pass.

It's one colossal mansion after another.

What real estate agents might call "bungalows" also perch on the hillsides which overlook the waking Valley. Do you know what the technical definition of a "bungalow" is? I looked it up once: "A one-story house, cottage, or cabin." There's no fucking way these are bungalows.

195. 197. 199. 201. 203 Carmella Drive.

My heart racing now.

I slow the Hummer to a crawl and drift past the mailbox of James Jansen. His house is a bungalow, set below the road, and from what I can tell, it commands a spectacular view of the Valley. Instead of stone, a wall of hedges hides his home from view.

I cruise on and pull over when the shoulder widens, a couple hundred yards down the hill from his mailbox.

My coffee's gone cool in the hour it's taken me to find Jansen's place.

I sit in the Hummer eating the bearclaw, as close as I've ever been to JJ.

To my knowledge, Jansen owns five homes: (1) a 12,000 square-foot log cabin in Montana; (2) this 5,000 square-foot bungalow in the Hollywood Hills, his primary residence; (3) a 5-bedroom apartment overlooking Central Park in Manhattan; (4) a three-story beach house in Nags Head on the Outer Banks of North Carolina; and (5) a villa in the South of France.

According to tabloids, rumors, Web sites, and everything else I've read about him in the last year, Jansen has not left LA in nine months. He hasn't worked on a project in three years, and his public and social appearances have been on the decline. He hasn't even been out in public (movie premiers, the Oscars, fundraisers…) since before Christmas. And people are beginning to wonder why. I won't even touch the speculation, but if his seclusion continues much longer, it will become a major story. But as of right now, his absence is only curious.

FAMOUS

In my rearview mirror, I can see Jansen's gate a little ways up the road. Since I have nothing to do now but wait, I lift Connor's script from the passenger seat.

It's done up quite professionally. The pages are bound with two brass brads, and the cover is heavy stock, protected by a sheet of plastic.

The screenplay is called *Until the End of Time*.

It's three hundred pages.

I turn to the first:

```
FADE IN:

Sunset over the Caribbean Sea.

EXT. BEACH - DAY

STEWART and BARBARA sit in the sand
watching the sunset. A pair of ducks
fly by, fucking in midair.

          STEWART

     Are you sure you're going to
     leave me?

          BARBARA

       (becoming misty)

     Yes, Stu. I've made my decision.
     And you won't talk me out of it.

          STEWART

     I'm so sad, Bar-bar.

          BARBARA

     I never meant to hurt you.
     That's the God's honest truth.

They kiss one last time as the screen
darkens.
```

The only reason I keep reading this horrid script is because there's nothing else to do.

The day slowly brightens all around me, and occasionally a jogger passes by. I wonder if they think I'm a private investigator or a bodyguard. This bright yellow Hummer isn't exactly what you'd call inconspicuous.

Since you're probably dying to know what happens in *Until the End of Time,* I won't keep you in suspense. Stewart, the lead, gets dumped by his wife on their honeymoon in the Caribbean. Understandably, he's devastated. He returns home to Chicago and goes back to work at the bank, making a concerted effort to get on with his life.

One day, while he's out to lunch, he happens to see his ex-wife in a restaurant. She's with a man, and Stu becomes very jealous. He follows them back to their house in the suburbs and learns that they have children together and have apparently been married for several years. Stewart breaks into their house and finds out that Bar-Bar is a Russian spy and the only reason she married him was because she thought he had access to top secret information.

At 10:35 a.m., a white Porsche emerges from Jansen's gate. I crank the Hummer as it peels out and tears down the street, doing better than sixty by the time it streaks past me. I follow along the winding trajectory of Carmella Drive, doing my best to keep up, but the Porsche is absolutely hauling ass. After several minutes, I think I've lost it, but I come around a curve and see the Porsche stopped in front of the slowly opening gate of a Santa Fe-style mansion. It disappears inside, and the gate closes me out.

I think I saw the back of Jansen's head. He was wearing a baseball cap.

A hundred yards down the street, I pull off the road again to wait.

I sit in the Hummer for four hours, and by three o'clock, I've got to pee something fierce. I imagine urinating on the side of the road will get you arrested pretty quick in a Star neighborhood. But I chance it, because my bladder is aching.

I feel much better climbing back behind the wheel.

Another four hours pass.

I call Kara, but she says she's cramming for an exam and to call her back tomorrow before noon. She hangs up quickly, almost like she wasn't thrilled that I took the time to call. I suppose she's just stressed. If we're going to get married, I have to learn to accept this intense side of her.

Since I've got my cell out, I call the fledgling screenwriter.

He answers: "Talk to me."

"Connor?"

"Yeah?"

"This is Jim Jansen. We met at Bo Bo's this—"

"Mr. Jansen! How are you?"

"I'm well. I've spent the morning reading your script." I pause for a moment. It's fun to mess with people. "And I absolutely…can you hold on one second?"

"Um, sure."

I put the phone down and stretch my arms. Man, it's toasty in this Hummer.

You may think it's mean, but I see it this way. Connor has zero talent, and he's never going to sell anything. He'll be a failure all of his life. Why not let him feel important and truly talented for a day or two. I pick up the phone again.

"Connor?"

"Yes."

"I love it."

"Really?"

"The writing is exceptional. I think we can do some business."

"Oh my God, are you kidding me?"

"Here's what's going to happen. I'm going to talk to some people this week, and get you a few meetings. You're going to pitch them with me attached, and I'll start hunting up a director. I've got a few in mind, but I want to think about it."

"Okay."

"Now, I want you to do something for me."

"What?"

"You and your friends go out and celebrate tonight."

Connor starts weeping.

"Mr. Jansen, you can't imagine what this means to me. I've dreamed my whole life of something like this, and now—"

The white Porsche pulls out onto the street.

"I got to go now, Conner."

I crank the engine and zoom off after Jansen. He certainly likes to speed.

I follow him down into West Hollywood, and on N. Highland Avenue, he stops at a red light.

I'm directly behind him. The top is down on his Porsche. He isn't wearing a hat anymore. His haircut is similar to mine, though maybe a little longer. In his rearview mirror, I see his deep dark shades.

When the light turns green, he punches it through the intersection, and I follow him at a comfortable distance up the 101 into Universal City.

He turns eventually, and I start to turn as well until I see his destination.

A guard waves him through Gate 4 of Universal Studios.

I'm still stopped in the middle of the road.

The car behind me beeps.

I head on up the street and park in a handicap space.

Chapter 18

famished ~ Mikey's Slice of Joy ~ The Brick Room ~ the jazz quartet ~ observes Jansen ~ Jansen requests "The Summer Wind" ~ Lance approaches the Star

JJ pulls out of Gate 4 at 7:25, and I follow him, miserably, back up into the hills. I haven't eaten anything since my bearclaw nearly twelve hours ago, and when he turns back into his driveway, disappearing behind yet another gate, I'm on the verge of abandoning my stakeout.

Fifteen minutes pass, and I've just decided to turn around and go home, when the white Porsche emerges from the gate and zips out again.

Once more, I follow him back down into the Valley.

JJ pulls off N. Fairfax into the parking lot of this place called The Brick Room. I park several spaces away and watch him walk quickly across the pavement and disappear inside. Everywhere Stars go, they always move fast because they're important. Their time is more valuable than ours. Yours, rather.

If I don't eat something immediately, I'm probably going to die. There's a pizza joint a couple blocks down, so I leave the Hummer and set out for the restaurant. I gas up on soda and several slices of the greasiest pepperoni pizza you've ever seen. The place is called Mikey's Slice of Joy. I think it's a high school hangout, because I'm far and away the oldest guy here. There's this table of a dozen teenagers near my booth. Very loud. Very entertaining. Rich, too. They keep saying things like "yeah, my Lexus is so filthy," or "I maxed out my Discover again."

I eat fast, because I don't want to lose JJ.

By 8:55, I'm walking down Fairfax again in the hot Pacific evening.

I run my fingers through my hair and eat a breath mint. The lights of this endless city have begun to wink on. I smile. JJ's white Porsche is still there.

The Brick Room is mostly empty tonight. It's a dim place. The bar's straight ahead, and a couple of televisions hang from the ceiling, though you can't hear them. On the left end of the room, there's a small stage. A jazz quartet is swinging through a song called "Black Coffee." The quartet consists of a guy playing a Fender Rhodes, another guy on stand-up bass, a woman on acoustic guitar, and another tall, pretty woman with short, black hair and a gorgeous voice.

There are booths, tables, and barstools. A few of the tables are occupied, as well as about half of the barstools. All of the booths are empty save one near the stage, where Jansen sits alone, watching the musicians. On his table sits a fifth of Absolut, an ice bucket, and a glass.

I approach the bar, and when the bartender notices me, he comes over and asks, "More ice, Jim?" I'm not quite sure what to say.

"Could I just get a beer?"

He looks over toward the booth where Jansen sits, sees him there, and then returns his gaze to me. His eyes have lost their reverence. He pulls me a pint of beer off the tap and charges me seven dollars for it.

I take my beer to a booth directly across the room from JJ and have myself a seat.

It doesn't feel real to be in the same room with him. I feel like I'm watching him in a movie, and that him sitting over there in that booth with his bottle of vodka is all a part of the story. But the story goes nowhere, because he just sits there, watching the jazz singer, oblivious to everything else. Plain life is pretty boring.

I could probably scream and he wouldn't look over. Stars are accustomed to people screaming at them. He doesn't even know I'm in the room.

I'll tell you how he sits. He sits with his back against the wall, his legs stretched out across the bench seat. He's dressed very obscurely. Blue jeans, hiking boots, a tight white polo shirt, buttons undone of course.

When the jazz quartet finishes a song, he always claps.

I steal glances at him for the next hour. Boy, he drinks a lot. He's already gone a third of the way through the bottle.

When the quartet finishes the set, the jazz singer tells the eight patrons, "We're going to take a short break, but we'll be back."

The three musicians head straight for the bar where they're probably getting comped. The singer has a seat on her stool and unscrews a bottle of water. While she drinks, she thumbs through several pages of sheet music.

JJ slides out of the booth and walks up to her. You can tell by the way he walks that he's very drunk, but that he's been very drunk enough times not to act very drunk. I guess you could call him a professional drunk. This is what he says to her:

"You're wonderful. I love your voice."

"Thank you," she smiles. You can tell she knows who he is. For a second, I thinks he's hitting on her, but then he pulls out his wallet, removes several fifties, and drops them in the open, velvet-lined guitar case.

"For the record, if you could do "The Summer Wind" it would make my night."

"Well, that's a guy's song, but I'll see what I can do."

She smiles, Jansen smiles, and then he returns to his booth and slides back in.

First song of the next set is "The Summer Wind."

The thing with Stars—they always get their way. People just want to please them.

I wait until Jansen is halfway through the bottle.

It's after eleven o'clock.

The jazz quartet is on its third, and what I imagine is, its final set. The Brick Room has nearly cleared out. It's just me, Jansen, this guy drinking martinis at the bar, and a semi-boisterous table on the other side of the room.

I stand. I probably don't have to elaborate on how insanely nervous I am. My beer remains untouched on the table. I hate beer. Tastes like liquid cardboard.

I cross the room, and Jansen doesn't even notice me until I slide into his booth right across from him and stretch my feet out on the seat, just like he sits.

Man, do we look like twins.

He just stares at me for a moment, eyes squinted, mouth open.

"Holy shit," he laughs. "I'm pretty fucked up right now, but I'm fairly confident you look exactly like me."

"It's not the vodka."

"What?"

"It's not the vodka. I do look like you."

"Did you have plastic surgery or something?"

"No." Probably wise not to mention the scar I gave myself.

The bartender is suddenly standing at our booth.

"Is this a guest, Jim, or should I show him the fucking door?"

JJ looks at the bartender, grins, and then looks at me. He's amused. I think Stars are often amused by nobodies.

"I'll leave if you want to be left alone," I say. "I just thought you'd—"

"No, stay. Bruce, we're all good here."

"Sure, Jim." Bruce stills glares at me like, *the fuck are you doing at his booth?* I just hate guys like that. You can tell he really wanted to show me the door. He's a very big, strong guy. I suppose if you spend that much time in the weight room, you live for the moments when you get to show people the door.

"Hey, Bruce!" I yell after he's started walking away. "I'll take an Absolut straight up."

He nods. You can tell he's super-pissed he has to get me a drink now.

When Bruce is gone, JJ says, "What do you want?"

"Nothing."

"You a reporter?"

"No."

He pulls a pack of cigarettes from his pocket, taps one out, brings it to his mouth. Wish I had a light for him.

"What's your name?" he asks.

"Lancelot."

"Cute. How'd you know?"

"What?"

He sighs and leans forward. "I'm not wearing a sign or anything. You read it somewhere?"

"No." I have no idea what he's talking about.

"She's great, isn't she?" He points to the jazz singer.

I don't even look. I can't take my eyes off him.

"You're pretty drunk, aren't you?" I ask.

"Not *too* drunk." He blows a mouthful of smoke toward my face.

"You've put down half that bottle."

"It's a light night."

I turn around and watch the jazz singer finish up the song. I don't hear her though. I don't hear anything. This doesn't feel real.

"We could be twins," he says. I smile. "What's that called?" he says.

"What?"

"When you look exactly like someone else but you aren't related to them?"

"A pretty strange fucking coincidence, I'd say."

He laughs. I've made JJ laugh.

Bruce the bartender brings me my glass of vodka.

"Ten dollars," he says.

I go for my wallet, but Jansen reaches forward and touches my wrist.

"I got it, Bruce."

Good thing, too. I'm down to my last thousand.

As Bruce walks away, I dip my hand into the bucket, lift out an ice cube and drop it into my glass. Jansen raises his.

"To you, Lancelot."

I raise my glass.

"To you, Jim."

We clink glasses.

I sip my Vodka.

Jansen throws his back and sets it down hard on the table. He leans back and watches the jazz singer.

I nurse my drink and try not to stare at him. I'm sitting across from this man I've fantasized being and knowing for five years, and do you know what I'm thinking? Nothing. I can't think of anything to say to him that wouldn't be worshipful fan bullshit: *What was it like winning the Oscar? What are you working on now? Who are your influences? How do you get into character? Which director do you most admire?* If I watched enough *Hollywood Starz!* or skimmed enough gossip columns, I could find the answers to those questions. Maybe just sitting here with him is enough. Maybe knowing that he has uttered my former name and looked into my eyes and bought me a vodka straight up with one cube of ice is sufficient.

"Lancelot," he says, finding my eyes. It's like looking at myself. The perfection of me.

"Yes?"

"Do you want to come home with me?"

Chapter 19

drives Jansen home in the Hummer ~ why Lancelot is out in Hollywood ~ into the bungalow ~ Chip & Bailey ~ Oscar ~ a proposition ~ in the room of mirrors ~ getting naked ~ head ~ Oscar: a weapon ~ calls Kara ~ on the patio, remembering

Because Jansen is fairly "tight" as they used to say, I offer to drive him home in the Hummer. He gives me directions, since I don't know where he lives. The warm night air floods over us, and Jansen sits back, unbuckled, eyes closed, a half-grin on his face. Seems like quite the carefree guy.

"What are you doing out here, Lancelot?" he asks as we cruise up some road called Carmella Drive. The Valley lights twinkle in the darkness below, and I feel happy and afraid. It's 12:02 a.m. on the best day of my entire life.

"I'm a screenwriter."

"No shit?" he says, but you can tell he's not very interested. "Written anything I might've heard of?"

"I did this art-house thing a couple years ago called 'Growing Old.'"

"Sure, I've heard of that."

You can tell people anything and they'll say they've heard of it, because honestly, who wants to admit they don't know something? You ought to try it some time. It's pretty funny.

I see his bungalow in the distance, and he tells me his place is just ahead. As I slow down to turn into the opening gate, he reaches over and strokes my face. I'm not too sure what I think about that, but I look over at him and smile anyway.

Jansen's driveway is very steep. It circles in front of the house and I park behind a silver Lotus. There's also an army green Land Rover Defender and an old Stingray Corvette.

We climb out of the Hummer and I follow Jansen across the walkway to the front door. It's cool up here. Wind rattles the bushes and shrubs.

Jansen unlocks the front door and I enter his home. He punches in the alarm code, says, "Lights." The living room appears. There are potted trees and long, curving furniture and leather and glass and sculptures and paintings. Even aquariums. Dogs bark somewhere in the house, and I hear their padded paws heading for us.

Two golden retrievers are suddenly at our feet, panting, squirming between our legs, licking my hands, and crying for joy.

"This is Bailey and Chip," he says. I kneel down and pet the dogs. They're highly friendly.

Then I follow Jansen through a living room into the plushest den I've ever seen. It's a long, windowless room with a tall ceiling. There's a screen at one end and a projector at the other. Couches and chairs and black leather beanbags fill the space between.

"Another vodka?" he asks from behind a bar at the back of the room.

"Sure. This is quite a place, Jim."

What a really dumb fucking thing to say. He knows it's quite a place. That's why he paid millions of dollars for it.

I realize suddenly that I'm standing in front of a glass case filled with plaques and statues. My eyes immediately fix upon the bright gold Oscar. Jansen brings my drink over. He hands it to me and opens the cabinet.

"Here." Hands me the statue, which is even heavier than you might imagine. It feels incredible to see my fingers wrapped around it. I can almost hear the applause.

"Was this the best night of your life?" I ask him.

"Sure was."

I see him staring at the statue. In this moment, I love him. I want to tell him what he means to me. The smell of his sweat, slightly sweetened with remnants of cologne, drifts over me.

"I want you to fuck me Lancelot."

I don't even consider it. I just ask, "Can I bring Oscar?"

He nods, sips his drink, and walks out of the room.

I follow him, holding my statue. We pass through a kitchen with a brick oven, and then move down a long, wide corridor. He takes off his shirt as he walks and throws it at me. Very toned for an alcoholic.

We turn a corner. He tugs his belt out of his jeans and steps out of his hiking boots.

We enter a small dark room. Jansen begins lighting candles in each corner. As their flames come to life, I see that the walls and ceiling are mirrored.

"This is my yoga room. Take off all your clothes," he tells me. I'm not homosexual, but I'll be honest. I'm aroused. I remove my shirt and kick off my shoes. The floor is covered with highly plush carpet, and there's a mattress fitted with black silk sheets in the center of the room. Jansen unbuttons his jeans and pushes them down his muscular legs. He steps out of them, kicks them into a corner. The way he stares at me is interesting. Very intense. Sultry even. He slides his blue boxer shorts off, and his member points at me. I can't help but look. This is JJ.

Jansen steps forward and unbuttons my jeans. He slides his hand into my pants, then pulls my slacks and briefs down together and drops to his knees.

I watch us in the mirror. It's the strangest, most beautiful thing I've ever seen.

It doesn't take me long, and then he's staring up at me, still on his knees, smiling.

I tighten my grip on Oscar and smash Jansen on top of his head.

He stumbles back, still conscious.

People don't drop in real life like they do in the movies.

You have to hit them again and again.

It's 1:00 a.m. when I step out onto my patio. You should see my view of the Valley, silent and shimmering below. I sit down in an Adirondack chair with a glass of vodka and my cell. I dial Kara's number, and she answers sleepily after five rings:

"Hello?"

"Kara, do you know who this is?"

"Jim. Hey. What time is—"

"I'm sorry to be calling you so late. I just got back from a long night and wanted to hear your voice. I've been thinking about you all day."

"I've been thinking about you, too." She sounds so tired, but I think she's glad I called.

"Did you get a dress for the premier tomorrow?"

"I bought one today."

"Can't wait to see you in it. Well, I know it's late. I don't want to keep you up."

"It's all right." She has a beautiful sleepy voice. I'm tempted to invite her over, but I'm sure she's much too tired.

"I'll pick you up tomorrow around five," I say.

"Okay." God, I want to tell her I love her.

"Night, Kara."

"Goodnight."

I'm exhausted, but I don't want to sleep yet. The night is warm and luscious, and I feel an intense love for everyone. I've got Oscar sitting between my legs, and it makes me reminisce about that wonderful night I received this award. When Henry Goodson started reading the nominees, I didn't even give myself a chance. I'm humble that way. People have told me that my acceptance speech was one of funniest, most charming in the history of the Academy Awards. It wasn't planned, but I can tell you, it came straight from my heart.

Being famous is the very best thing in the world. I wish you knew.

Chapter 20

wakes up happy ~ listens to the message ~ breakfast on the patio ~ the spider web ~ a walkthrough of his new bungalow ~ a cancellation ~ takes a bath ~ returns the Hummer ~ fun in a Porsche ~ the screenplay he's writing ~ Ravenous Games ~ Lance for the last time ~ goodbye to Bo at the fountain

Sunlight spills through my bedroom window. I stretch and kick off the blankets.

From my pillow, I can see morning in the Valley.

The sky is an early blue.

I climb out of bed.

My master suite is enormous. There's a treadmill by one of the windows.

You wouldn't believe the size of my closet. I step inside and choose a robe. It's black satin—very suave.

As I walk down the hallway toward the kitchen, the phone rings. I let it go. It's only 8:15—much too early to be answering the phone.

While I peruse the fridge for fruit and orange juice, the answering machine picks up.

"This is Jim. Leave a message and do keep in mind that brevity is the soul of wit."

I pour a glassful of juice. It's organic.

"Hey, Jim, I was thinking, you remember that scene we wrote involving Bernard and the hooker? Bring it with you, since you're holding onto all the drafts. At least I hope you are. It might actually work if we put it after Bernard leaves the Christmas party. I don't know. Just a thought. See you at ten."

I have a pleasant breakfast on the patio. It's still misty up here in the hills. Very cool and refreshing. When I finish the cantaloupe, I just sit back in that Adirondack chair, basking.

On a tree several yards down the hill, I notice this massive spider web. You wouldn't believe it if you saw it. I mean, the thing stretches five or six feet between the branches. And in the middle of it, this spider just sits there, waiting, stoic. The sun burning through the mist makes the silk web glisten. As I sit there looking at this marvel of nature, it occurs to me: *this is as much sense as anything ever makes.* I am intensely moved by a spider web. I'm happy about being happy about a spider web.

After breakfast, I take a tour of my bungalow—the home theatre, the living room, the kitchen, dining room, hallway, and three spare bedrooms, and the master suite.

I don't bother with the room of mirrors.

In a corner of my bedroom, there's a desk, and in the drawers I find everything I need. Wallet, car keys, BlackBerry account information, bank statements (I am so fucking rich!), contracts…

It turns out that I'm currently writing a screenplay with the actor Brad Morton. (He's been in a whole slew of movies. His most famous was *The Golftress* about this guy who's a mediocre professional golfer and undergoes a sex change operation so he can play on the Ladies' PGA tour. It's one of the funniest movies you'll ever see. Morton's garnered a couple Golden Globes, but no Oscar. I'm sure I hold this over his head at every opportunity).

Morton's phone number is in my BlackBerry, and I call him up, sounding very sickly and tired, like I've been throwing up all night. He offers to come over and make me some chicken soup, but I tell him not to bother. I'd probably just puke it up anyway. He asks if it's a hangover, and I tell him "a vicious one."

I take a bath in my garden tub and test myself on my PIN number for my bank account, my social security number, the alarm code, my address, and date of birth. It's always good to keep these things fresh in mind.

I can see the Valley while splashing in the tub.

After my bath, I choose an outfit for the day.

As it turns out, I'm a big fan of black silk. My closet is full of it, so I go with black leather pants, a black silk short-sleeved button-up, and these interesting crocodile shoes which raise me an inch and a half.

I set the alarm and lock up the house.

It's 10:30 in the morning.

I drive the Hummer back to Exotic Car Rentals of Beverly Hills, turn it in, recover my deposit.

Then I call a cab and have the driver take me to the Brick Room.

Thank God my Porsche is still there. I lower the top and peel out onto Fairfax.

Man, this car is a kick to drive. I like it even more than the Hummer. It's so fast and low to the ground. Just for fun, I take it out on I-10 and scream toward the ocean.

I have lunch at the bungalow and read through the latest draft of Brad's and my screenplay. It's called *The Great Wide Open*, and I have no idea what it's about. The only thing that really happens in the first twenty pages is this guy named Bernard finds out that his newest wife is cheating on him with his son, and then he sort of has a mental meltdown in a bathroom. One minute, he's washing his hands, the next, he's beating up an electric hand dryer. It's pretty funny. I'm a very good writer.

Since I have several hours before the movie premiere, I drive down to Century City.

Ravenous Games occupies a suite in this office building across the street from 20th Century Fox Studios.

I ride the elevator to the fourth floor and walk down the drab, impersonal hallway. It doesn't even have the name of his company on the door.

Bo's office is incredibly messy. There are no windows. The walls are covered with posters advertising videogames with names like *Blood Bath XII—The Reckoning*.

Bo sits in front of a television playing a videogame. I'm sure he doesn't get paid to do this. He's so focused on the game, he doesn't hear me walk in.

"You're telling me you get paid to play videogames?" I ask.

Bo pauses the game and looks over his shoulder.

"What's up, Lance?" Fuck, I hate that.

"Just thought I'd stop by. See where you work."

"You're looking at it."

"What are you working on right there?"

"Just testing a late phase of this first-person shooter. Look, I hate to be this way, but I am insanely busy."

"Oh, I'm sorry, I didn't—"

"Could we talk tonight? I was thinking of grilling a few steaks."

I lean against the doorframe. On the paused television screen, a samurai warrior is on his knees. Another samurai is swinging a huge sword at his head, which will undoubtedly roll when Bo resumes the game.

"I won't be here tonight," I say. "I'm leaving."

"When?"

"Right now. I came to tell you goodbye."

Bo turns the videogame off and stands.

"Let's go outside."

Bo's office building is one of four in a small business park called the Quadrangle. In the courtyard between the buildings, there's a manmade pond with a fountain in the middle. Swans sail through its green water.

We sit down on a bench near the water. It's two-thirty and very hot. Someone sits by themselves on an identical bench across the pond, reading a book and eating lunch.

Bo asks me where I'm going, and I tell him that I don't know for sure. I'm considering taking what money I've got left, buying a used car, and driving down into Mexico.

"What's in Mexico?" he asks.

"I don't know. Desert, ocean, tacos. I've always wanted to go." This is true. I have always been intrigued by its wildness.

"You have to leave this afternoon? Why can't you stay with us a little longer. I love having you here."

"You do?"

"Yes."

"Hannah doesn't."

"Fuck her. You're my brother."

I pat Bo on the shoulder, and then something happens that I never even expected. I start to cry. Not weeping or anything, just tears rolling down my cheeks.

"I'm going to miss you very much," I say.

Bo squeezes the back of my neck.

"I'm sorry about what I said the other night, Bo."

He smiles. "Don't be."

"No, I should never have—"

"It's fine. Look, I thought a lot about our talk out on the soccer field. Especially after I never saw you yesterday, and you didn't come home last night." Bo looks at me the way only he looks at me. Sometimes, I think he's the only person in the world who loves me. "I don't know what's going on with you right now, Lance. I don't know why you came out here. Why you're leaving now. I love you. You know that. You know that?"

I nod yes.

"Maybe I'm off base here, but I'm just going to say it. And I say this in love. You seem to me like a man who's lost his bearings. You come out here, you buy flashy clothes." He motions to my beautiful leather pants. "You rent a Hummer, you do the nightclub thing. I don't understand where you're at, Lance, but if I can help you in any way—money, a place to stay, finding a job, whatever—please let me. The other night, I sort of made it sound like my boring suburban life is the only way. I know it's not. I know it's probably not for you. And I'm sorry I pulled that shit on you."

I smile at my brother.

"I envy your life, Bo. No, I envy your ability to love it. To let it settle you. "

"You're not at peace are you?"

"No. But I'm getting there. I honestly am."

And I start to tell him about the spider web, but I stop myself. I don't think I could bear him not getting it.

Chapter 21

*Rex saves the day ~ looking fabulous ~ picks up Kara
~ quells her fear ~ on the Red Carpet ~ talks with
Entertainment Magazine ~ Harvey Wallison ~ The
Action ~ the scene that made Jim cry*

At 4:30, I realize I haven't called the limousine service. I don't know if you've noticed, but Stars don't step out onto the Red Carpet from their Hondas. In my BlackBerry, there's a number for Rex Smothers with "limo" in parentheses beside the name. I call up Rex and tell him I'd forgotten to call him, but that I'm attending the premier of Richard Haneline's new movie at the El Capitan Theatre tonight and would give him any amount of money if he could pick me up at my place in one hour.

Sure he can. Rex is a hell of a guy.

I don't go the traditional tuxedo route (we'll save that for the Oscars). Several years ago, I wore this slick gray Armani to the premier of *Under the Sea*. I find that very suit hanging on a row of two dozen Armanis, and it puts a smile on my face like you wouldn't believe.

I shave, style my hair, and put on a touch of eyeliner. Honestly, I've never looked so good. It's frightening. There's a change now in my eyes, too. A calm, blue confidence.

Kara's waiting in the lobby of her apartment building when Rex pulls up in the black limo. I step out and hold the door for her. Man, she's beautiful. I tell her so. She's wearing a chiffon evening dress, which is such a deep shade of green it could be black.

We climb in and we're off. Rex looks back and tells us we'll be at the theatre in ten minutes. He's a small, black man. You can hardly see him over the steering wheel.

"It's so good to see you," I tell Kara.

"I'm scared, Jim."

I pull her close to me and take a whiff of her hair. I stroke her bare shoulder.

"Are people going to ask who I am?"

"They might."

"I don't know if I can do this."

"Look at me." She looks at me. "I've done this so many times it's boring. You're with *me* tonight. No one's going to bother you. If a reporter happens to ask you something inappropriate, I'll be right there beside you. Besides, all the questions will probably come at me anyway." I kiss her forehead. "Just smile and enjoy it. You're going to be famous tonight, Kara."

"I don't want to be famous, Jim. I just want to be with you."

Richard Haneline's new movie is called *The Action*, and from the previews I've seen, I have to say it actually looks halfway decent. It's apparently about this degenerate gambler who takes out a second mortgage on his house, cashes in his kids' college savings, and sneaks off to Vegas. It's good to see Rich starring in a character-driven movie. If I have to watch him blow up one more thing, I'm seriously not going to be his friend anymore.

The clock on the dashboard reads 6:40 when Rex stops the limousine at the Red Carpet and opens his door. As he walks around to open the door for us, I look at Kara and kiss her on the lips.

She squeezes my hand.

"If you move more than two feet away from me at any time this evening, I'll kill you, Jim."

Beyond the tinted glass, I see swarms of people. I put on my deep dark shades.

Rex opens our door. My heart throbs like a migraine, but I smile through it and step out of the limousine onto the blood-Red Carpet. These are the things I will always remember:

-The brilliant evening sun.

-The roar of fans screaming from the bleachers.

-The van-size dice hanging above the theatre entrance.

-Flashbulbs going off like machinegun fire.

-A wave of weightlessness, as though I'm on the verge of floating up into the sky.

-Kara's sweaty hand gripping mine as she steps out of the limo.

"Are we going, Jim? Why aren't we moving?" I hear her, but I'm not ready to move yet. I'm looking down at the ground, at that beautiful Red Carpet beneath my mirror-black shoes. Have you ever stood on Red Carpet that's been rolled out exclusively for you? It means you're too important to walk on the pavement. Normal people can walk on pavement but not you. You're better. You're special. That's the implication, and it feels so good.

No one can ever take this moment away from me.

I look up into the bleachers. Fans are waving and shouting my name. I smile the smuggest, coolest smile you've ever seen and wave back at them.

We begin to walk. The carpet ahead of us is crowded with Stars and normal people involved in the production of *The Action*.

"James, please! I love you!" This girl literally screams. She's on the front row behind the metal railing, holding out a notepad. I walk toward her, and the crowd squeezes in, crushing her up against the bars.

"Could I have an autograph, Mr. Jansen?"

"Of course you can." I release Kara's hand and take the pen and pad. "What's your name?"

"Bethany."

I scribble down, "To Bethany, Love, James Jansen."

"Can I have a kiss on the cheek, too? I could die happy."

She's probably twenty or twenty-one. She's not a knockout or anything, but I'm feeling pretty generous, so I plant one on her cheek. She and everyone around her commence screaming. I wave up to the crowd above their heads, shout, "I love you!" and then Kara and I walk on.

"You're very good at this, Jim," she whispers, as we approach a woman with a microphone standing in front of a camera. "You should feel my heart. It's just racing."

The woman with the microphone spins around as we pass by.

She's one of the anchors for *Hollywood Starz!*. She wears a highly glittery dress.

"Look who it is," she tells the camera, "Oscar-winner James Jansen."

I stop walking and stand beside the reporter. I think her name is Marcy Meyers, but I'm not certain. When you're a Star, you have to talk to the reporters. It's sort of a rule.

"How are you doing tonight, Jim? You look fabulous!" She puts her hand on my shoulder.

"So do you." Always complement the female reporters. It's easy with Marcy, because she honestly looks exceedingly hot.

"So are you guys looking forward to seeing the movie?" No, I think it's going to be a steaming pile. Ever notice how reporters, for the most part, ask blazingly stupid questions?

"Oh absolutely. I think Rich has worked some magic in this film."

"That's certainly the buzz, isn't it? And you look beautiful, too," Marcy tells Kara. I squeeze Kara's hand, and she smiles gracefully.

"Thank you."

I can see in Marcy's eyes that she wants to ask Kara something, but she backs off.

"So, Jim, when are we going to be standing at *your* premier? Not too much longer I hope."

Right, like I'm going to tell you first. You have to be very careful how you answer that sort of question, because if you say the wrong thing, or even the right thing with less than perfect ambiguity, you'll wind up in the tabloids.

"Things are in the works, Marcy, and that's all I can say at this point."

"Oh, come on, Jim! You're teasing us!"

I smile that winning, this-conversation-is-over smile.

"Well, thanks for stopping by to chat with us. You guys enjoy the movie."

As we walk away, I wonder if two people are sitting in Huntersville, North Carolina at this moment, on an old, stinky couch, in a house that smells like cabbage. The man is soused up pretty good on cheap gin, the woman thinking about Jesus, and neither of them realize who just strolled across their television screen.

To the households that watch us, we are nothing more than glorious, enviable constellations. We're symbols of perfection. Charismatic gods. I'm beginning to understand how necessary we are.

We're drifting through the lobby of the El Capitan, when this guy in a tux steps right in front of us with a big, goofy smile on his face. He wears thick, black-rimmed glasses, and his hair is black and curly.

"Jim! What's going on?"

I smile, guardedly.

"Hey, there," I say. "Good to see you."

"Great to see you. Look, are you going to Rich's afterward?"

"I think we're planning on it."

"Great, because I want to talk with you about something. It's a project that's in development, and I'd love to tell you about it. I think it'd be perfect for you."

"Sounds good."

"And nice to see you," he says to Kara. "I don't think we've met."

"Kara Suthers," she says, extending her hand.

"Harvey Wallison. A real pleasure. Well, you guys enjoy the movie, and we'll talk later, Jim."

When Kara and I have taken our seats in the theatre, she leans over and whispers into my ear: "Who was that man?"

"You mean Harvey Wallison? You haven't heard of him?"

"Should I have?"

"He's a brilliant director. Did *Down From the Sleeping Trees*, and if you tell me you haven't heard of that, I'll take you home right now." I smile to let her know I'm only kidding. She smiles back, and as the lights go down, we kiss.

The Action, I'm delighted to say, is one of the best movies I've seen in a long, long time. Rich's performance as Wally Miller may very well earn him an Oscar nomination. I even mist up, and as a rule, movies never make me cry. The scene that got me happens toward the end of the movie. Wally has blown the last of his $110,000 dollars at the blackjack table, and he sort of has a meltdown in the casino. It's very poignant, as they say. He crumples down on the floor and just starts wailing, and practically everyone in the casino is staring at him. Then this lady walks over to him, kneels down, and gives him a $1,000-dollar chip. Wally looks up at her and says, "I can't do it anymore. I just can't." I'm telling you, everyone in the theatre lost it at the same moment. Then Wally starts crying again, and the pit boss has security drag him out of the casino.

Everybody's mascara is running as they leave the theatre. And it's quiet, too, like we're coming out of church on Good Friday. I've got a feeling that when the reporters ask the Stars what they thought of the movie, and everyone raves about how wonderful it was, this is one of the rare times they'll mean it.

Chapter 22

misgivings ~ Santa Monica Pier ~ the trouble with perfection ~ arrives at the mansion of Richard Haneline ~ greets the host ~ the view no one sees ~ goes to get drinks ~ the finger wave ~ a strange encounter

We have a couple hours before Rich Haneline's party, since the studio is throwing a bash at the Roosevelt directly following the premiere. And I'm sure we're on the guest list and all, but I've got to tell you, I'm feeling a tad nervous about the prospect of mingling with hundreds of Stars and industry types who I'm supposed to know, some very well, most at least superficially.

It feels wonderful and safe when Kara and I are back in the limousine and Rex is driving us south out of Hollywood toward a surprise destination.

"That was amazing," she tells me. "I mean, Jan Bollinger shook my hand and told me she loved my dress. I know that's probably no big deal for you, but you have to understand, I've watched her movies all my life. She's going to Richard's party. She told me, 'I'll see you there.' This is so much fun, Jim."

We reach our surprise destination, and Rex gets out and opens the door for us.

"What are we doing here?" Kara asks.

"I thought it'd be nice to kill an hour or two watching the sunset."

"And here's what you asked for," Rex says, handing me a small cooler.

Rex is a wonderful driver. While we watched the movie, he went out and purchased champagne at my request.

It's 8:30, and if I squint and measure with my thumb and index finger, the sun is roughly an inch above the horizon of calm blue ocean.

Kara and I walk onto the Santa Monica Pier.

We stroll all the way to the end and only pass three people—a starry-eyed couple, and an old man, fishing.

We have the end of the pier all to ourselves, and we sit down on a bench and watch the sun sink into the sea.

I open the cooler, remove the bottle of champagne and two plastic flutes.

"Look at you," Kara says as I work out the cork.

It pops off, clears the railing, gone.

To tell you the truth, I'm kind of sad as I pour the champagne. It's like what I realized that morning in New York. Sometimes, things are so perfect, you know it can't get any better. The most tragic point of existence isn't when you've bottomed out. It's when you've peaked, when you've just crested perfection and can see it beginning to fall away in your rearview mirror.

"To you, Kara."

"To you, Jim."

Part of me wants to skip Rich's party and go home.

"What's wrong," Kara asks me.

"I'm very happy right now."

She giggles.

"That's a bad thing?"

I take a sip of the champagne. Very spritzy. I look at Kara, her short blond hair pulled behind her ears except for a few wisps which hang down over her eyes. I brush them back for her.

"I don't see how it could get any better," I say.

"That's so sweet."

She leans forward and kisses me and puts her head on my shoulder.

But I wasn't trying to be sweet. I understand that she thinks I was implying that being here with her is a surreal experience (and it is) but that's not what I really meant. I genuinely don't think this night can get any better, and as such, I'd rather not go to Rich's party.

I finish my champagne and set the flute down and caress Kara's shoulder.

"Sure you're up for this party?" I say. "We could just go back to my place."

"That's sweet of you, but I think I can handle it now. Maybe I'll even let you stray three or four feet away from me this time." She laughs again and pinches my arm. I laugh, too, but it's forced.

I am so uneasy.

The sun is halfway into the ocean. Then three quarters. Then only a sliver remains. Then it's gone.

We sit for awhile in the dark.

Rich's mansion is on top of this hill that overlooks the sea. We cruise by the house at 10:15, but through the gate, it looks as though only several limos are parked in the huge circular drive.

So Rex drives us up and down the Pacific Coast Highway, and at a quarter past eleven, we re-arrive at the Haneline's. Now, there's a line to get through the gate, and we feel confident the party is in full swing.

As Rex pulls into the line of cars dropping off guests at the front door, I count thirty-six limos. When it's our turn, Rex opens our door, and I help Kara out of the backseat. I can smell the ocean, hear the assault of waves in the darkness below the hill.

Rich and Margot stand by the massive, intricately-carved door (I read somewhere that the front door alone cost half a million dollars) to their 17,000 square-foot home (a reported $29,000,000), beneath the porch light, greeting their guests. Rich looks almost stately in his tuxedo. His wife, Margot, can't be more than thirty. She's stunning. Perhaps the first trophy wife I've seen in real life.

"Jim!" he smiles when we reach the top of the steps. We embrace, do some good old fashioned back-slapping, and then pull back to look at each other, arms still entwined.

"I am so glad you could make it," he tells me.

"Can I make a prediction?" I say. "Oscar nom." I poke his chest. "You were brilliant, Rich. You've outdone yourself this time."

"I appreciate that. And who is this?" he gestures to Kara.

"Rich, meet Kara."

"Kara," he takes her hand, "it is such a pleasure to meet you. I'm thrilled you could come. This is Margot."

Margot smiles and steps forward in a glittering white evening dress. She shakes Kara's hand, then looks at me. This may sound crazy, but from the way she looks at me, I think we may have something going on.

"Jim," she extends her hand, and I take it, exactly like Rich took Kara's, "does he have to make a movie for you to come to our house?"

"Of course not." I smile. "But it helps." Winning smile. Laughs all around.

Rich tells us to go on in and he'll be along shortly.

As Kara and I step through the monstrous front door, I get the feeling that Rich and I used to be very close. I wish I could remember what happened. I should probably tell my doctor about this awful amnesia.

You wouldn't believe that someone actually lives in this palace. You walk through the front door into this gardened atrium. Whole trees are growing out of the floor, and up above, these skylights let moonlight in.

We pass through the atrium, where guests mingle, sipping drinks by candlelight and moonlight. Staircases curve up on either side and meet at the second floor, where four large oil paintings adorn the wall. They each have their own lighting system, so even though the hallway is dark, they seem to glow.

Beyond the atrium, we enter a long family room with fireplaces on either end so tall I could stand up inside them. The kitchen shines beneath inlay lighting—steel appliances, black marble countertops, and a brick oven that puts mine to shame.

We hear the music as we approach French doors leading out onto the veranda. A server opens the door for us, and placing my palm on the small of her back, I lead Kara out into the eye of the party.

When she sees the view, she whispers, "My God."

The veranda of Rich's mansion is like nothing I've ever seen. It runs the length of the house, and at fifty feet wide, it's crowded with partygoers, a jazz band, three bars, a life-size bull made out of butter, a chocolate fountain, and several tables of exquisite hors d'oeuvre.

Kara practically drags me over to the stone railing. It comes to our waists, and we lean against it and look straight down seventy-five feet to a rocky beach. The moon has just begun to silver the inky sea, and we stand watching the waves far below, and gazing up and down the Malibu coast, at the lights of other cliff-top mansions.

It's kind of funny. No one else at the party seems even halfway enchanted with the extraordinary view. I mean, this is one of the most beautiful things Kara and I have ever seen, and no one really cares.

"No one else even sees this," I whisper.

"What?" The sea breeze stirs her hair.

"This view. They might as well be in some stuffy room. Do you see it?"

"I see it. And I see you."

I stare into her eyes, dark jewels.

"You want to dance?" I ask her.

"No."

"What do you want to do?"

"Go home with you."

"That can be arranged." We laugh, and touch noses, and kiss.

"I'm going to get a drink," I tell her. "Can I bring you back something?"

"Glass of white wine would be nice."

"Okay. You'll be here?"

"Right here."

I make my way toward the nearest bar, avoiding eye contact with anyone. I order my specialty and a glass of white for Kara, and while the bartender fixes the drinks, I survey the crowd, not recognizing as many faces as I thought I might. Jan Bollinger, the actress, is dancing with a tall, Italian man who can't be more than twenty-two. She's fifty-five, by the way. She does a little finger-wave to me. I finger-wave back.

"Here you are, sir." The bartender hands me my drinks.

I try to tip him, but he won't accept my money.

As I start to walk away, someone grabs my arm, and I nearly drop the glasses.

A youngish man, maybe twenty-five, stares angrily into my eyes. He's still holding my arm. He wears a black, silk shirt and leather pants, similar to what I might sport when I go clubbing with the commoners.

"There a problem?" I say.

He gets right up into my face, whispers, "Least you can do is mail it back."

"I don't know what you're talking about." He brushes his hair out of his eyes. His face is tan, angular.

"I'll bet. What are you afraid I'll spill it here? That ain't going to happen."

"If you don't let go of my arm, I'm going to throw you over the fucking cliff."

He lets go of my arm.

"I'm sorry," he says. "I shouldn't…I let my temper get away from me." He fixes his collar, takes a deep breath. Smoothes his hair. "I guess should just be thrilled that the great James Jansen let me suck him off in a prop closet," he says, a little loud for comfort. "You didn't have to feign interest in my script, you know."

FAMOUS

Now I step into the young man's face.

"I don't know how you got in to this party, but if you ever speak to me again, I'll have you run out of this town."

He looks pretty scared when I say this, so I must've played it right. I turn and walk toward Kara without looking back, though I can feel his eyes on me, and my heart going like mad.

Chapter 23

Margot and Kara view the Manet ~ Jim's vodka commits suicide ~ gets pitched by Harvey Wallison ~ feeling pretty shitty

Rich and Margot are talking with Kara when I return with her wine, and she's telling them all about her studies in the art program at UCLA. She's very engaging. Rich and Margot talk to interesting people all the time, and I'm telling you, they're riveted.

"Well, you need to come up and see out Manet," Margot says.

"You have a Manet?"

"Oh, it's breathtaking. If you looked up toward the second-floor hallway when you first came in, you'd have seen it. Come on! Let me show you!"

Kara looks at me, glowing, and takes her wine.

"Gentlemen," Margot says, taking my date by the arm. "Think you can entertain yourselves while we're gone?"

The ladies head off through the crowd toward the house.

Rich and I lean against the railing and stare out to sea. A mile out, a yacht cruises off the coast.

"She's adorable, Jim," Rich tells me. "Where'd you two meet?"

"At La Casa actually. Night I saw you there."

"Oh, a new romance." He sips what appears to be a Perrier.

Somewhere in the crowd behind us, a woman screams: "Oh, go to hell!"

"So what's up with that?" Rich points to the glass in my hand.

"What, this?"

"Yeah, that."

"It's just a vodka with—"

"Look, maybe it's not my place, but…" He doesn't finish the thought.

"What?"

"You're going to kill yourself. Let me have that."

"Are you kidding?"

He takes my glass and throws it over the railing.

Two seconds, and I hear it shatter on the rocks below.

I'm not sure what to say, so I don't say anything.

"How's the script coming?" he asks.

"It's coming."

"Yeah? You going to star?"

"Who else? You?"

"Hey, come next March, I might be the hottest ticket in town."

"I sincerely hope so."

Rich finishes off his Perrier. "You want one of these? I'm going to go for another."

"No thanks."

Rich adjusts his bowtie and sort of just takes me in.

"I don't know what it is, Jim, but you seem different somehow."

My stomach comes up my throat.

"What do you mean?"

"I don't know. Maybe it's the girl, but you seem more grounded. At peace even."

"Wouldn't that be something?"

Kara doesn't come back for awhile, so I meander through the crowd, back toward the jazz band at the other end of the veranda. I bump into a few people who know me along the way, and one of them, an agent, goes on and on about how she read a *New York Times* rave review for some off-off-Broadway thing I did, and how she had no idea I had stage chops.

It's easier than you might think talking to someone you don't remember. Because if you let them, most people will talk exclusively about themselves. Honestly, they don't really want to know how you're doing. And if they do ask, it's merely out of courtesy, and they won't be listening to your answer. They'll be nodding their head, smiling at you, and wondering, *Do I have something in my teeth? I wonder if John's here. Oh, there's Mary! I need another drink.*

Practically everyone asks about the screenplay Brad Morton and I are writing. Some people seem to have read portions of it. I'm telling you, there's a buzz. Everyone asks me where Brad is, like I'm supposed to be keeping tabs on him or something. I hate that. I don't know what I'm going to do about Brad. I really don't.

The jazz band is smoking. Especially the drummer. He's one cool cat as they say. The only thing that moves are his arms. The rest of his body is perfectly still, and he just stares out at the ocean while he plays these blistering fills, like he could give a shit who he's playing for.

When I glance through the crowd again, I see Harvey Wallison making his way toward me. We haven't made eye contact, and since he doesn't know I've seen him, I walk through the French doors, into Rich's house, moving quickly through the kitchen, a ridiculous dining room, with a table that could seat forty guests, and finally arriving at the atrium. There's a chair beside this gurgling fountain, so I sit down and cross my legs and wait, praying Harvey doesn't see me.

Shortly thereafter, he comes around the corner from the dining room and stops, looking over the candlelit atrium and the half dozen people who occupy its chairs and sofas. I'm hoping he won't recognize me in the lowlight of the candles, but when he looks in my direction, he smiles and starts toward me.

He sits down in the empty chair across from mine, takes out a handkerchief, pats down his forehead.

"I hate these things," he says. "Wear me the fuck out."

He sips from his glass of Scotch and sets it on the wrought iron table betwixt us.

"Good to see you out again, Jim."

"Good to be out."

"Yeah? You feeling well?"

"I think so. Some people tell me I seem different." He nods, touching his index finger to the corner of his eye. I think Harvey might be one of those rare listeners. "I feel different," I say.

"Well, you're sort of just getting back into the swing of things."

"Yeah."

"And I think it's terrific that you are, Jim. You're a helluva brave soul, and a lot of people are rooting for you."

I pat Harvey on the knee.

Harvey sips his Scotch and removes his glasses.

"I don't know what your timetable is for picking your next project. I'll tell you, Guy Watson and Tyler Law are hounding me for this part. I've had both of them over to read with Lauren and it was good. I'm not going to say it wasn't. But it wasn't what it could be."

"What do you mean?"

He looks me hard in the eyes. "Jim, I've only worked with you on one film, but I know when something's perfect for you, and buddy, this is it. A role like this comes along once, maybe twice in a man's career."

He leans in closer. I can smell the single malt on his breath.

"I know I'm coming on strong here, Jim, and believe me, I don't want you to do this if you aren't ready, or if you don't want it. But if any part of you is interested, I would urge you to come up to my place for a read. I won't lie to you. I want you at least partly for selfish reasons. I think you'd make this film the best thing I've ever done. I think you'd make it a classic. But as much as I want these things for me, I want them also for you."

He finishes his Scotch, and I'm wondering if I'm already supposed to know the premise.

I take a chance.

"So what's it about, Harvey? I apologize, you may have already told me."

Harvey gets up and stands in front of me.

I am very uncomfortable.

I keep waiting for him to ask me something I don't know.

"You're a car salesman in the Midwest. A family man. You have a wife and daughter. You come home early from work one day to surprise your wife and find her in bed with your next door neighbor, Michael. You sit outside the door and listen to them making wild, flagrant love."

He takes a breath and half-grins at me like, *Are you hooked yet?*

And I guess I am. It's a fairly intriguing premise.

"That night, about two in the morning, you sneak over to your neighbor's house and murder him and bury him in his backyard. His wife and children are visiting family in another state.

"The next hour and forty-five minutes chronicles Michael's body being discovered your wife's growing suspicion that you murdered him, and your own deteriorating mental state brought on by an ocean of guilt. It's called *Next Door*."

He's smiling. I am, too.

I say, "Wow."

"Yeah?"

"Harvey, I want to see this movie."

"See it? Star in the motherfucker!"

I take a deep breath. I think the only way Harvey's going to leave me alone is if I agree to do a reading.

"All right. I'll read with Lauren." I don't even know which Lauren he's talking about.

"Really?" I don't think he expected me to agree.

"Well, you hooked me."

Harvey kneels down and hugs my legs. It's sort of embarrassing.

Heading back toward my place, Kara puts her hand on the back of my neck and runs her fingers through my hair.

"What's wrong, Jim?" she asks.

I don't turn around. I don't say anything.

She snuggles close to me, so that when she speaks, I feel her warm, moist breath on my ear.

"Did something happen at the party?"

"Harvey Wallison wants me to star in his new movie."

"That's great!"

"Everyone wants to know how my screenplay is coming along. They can't wait to read it."

"That's wonderful!"

Our limo is winding up Laurel Canyon. The road is very steep. If Rex were to make a steering mistake, we'd go plunging down into a ravine.

"These things aren't wonderful," I say, still gazing out the window.

"Why?"

"Everyone wants things from me."

"Well, isn't that—"

"What if I can't deliver?"

"What do you mean?"

"What if I can't do the things these people want?"

"But you can, Jim. You're a brilliant actor. I know. I've seen your films. You've won an Oscar, for Chrissakes."

It's two a.m., and I'm so angry. It even surpasses the fear.

There's nothing like getting exactly what you want and it still not being enough.

Chapter 24

*with Kara in the bungalow ~ Kara holds the Oscar
~ Margot's curiosity ~ the angry goldens ~ the worst
thing that can possibly happen when you're making
love to a woman (it's not what you think) ~ finishes
the job ~ finishes the other job ~ Kara takes the
Defender ~ digs a hole ~ the Star Wars analogy*

Even though we just came from the mansion to end all mansions, Kara's pretty blown away by my bungalow. I take her inside and give her the quick tour. She seems particularly enthralled with my home theatre.

"You have to have me over to watch a movie some time," she says. Of course that won't happen. I've decided now, but I smile just the same and say that of course we will. We'll pop popcorn and do the whole shebang.

Kara spends a moment staring at Oscar.

I open the case for her and let her hold it. I see flakes of dried blood in the crevices, but they're microscopic. I'm sure she won't notice.

"It's so heavy," she tells me.

"That's what everyone says."

"Was this like the best night of your life?"

"It was."

I fix her a drink (Crown and Coke, very easy on the Crown) and take her out onto the patio. After the obligatory drooling over my extraordinary view of Los Angeles, we settle back into Adirondack chairs and talk superficially about the Haneline party and our interactions with various guests.

Then Kara mentions her conversation with Margot.

"Yeah, Margot was pretty interested in you," Kara tells me.

"What do you mean?"

"Oh, she was just asking how you'd been doing and all."

"Been doing with what?"

"You know."

"No, Kara, I don't know."

"With the uh…the substance abuse thing," she whispers the last part.

"Oh. Thank you, Margot."

"Jim, it's fine. None of my business. I don't care."

"You don't care if I'm a drug addict?"

She sighs, and I can tell by the way she plays with her ice that she'd love to have a second crack at not bumbling into this topic.

"Of course I care," she says finally.

I reach over and take hold of her hand which is wet and cold from holding the Crown and Coke.

"I'm doing much, much better," I tell her. "You should know that I went through some hard times a while back, but that I've come through it. I'm healthy now, Kara."

It's not much fun admitting to being a drunk and/or drug addict when you're not, but I guess you've got to make sacrifices sometimes.

"You want to go inside?" I ask, and yes, I'm asking exactly what you think I'm asking.

"Love to," she replies, and by the way her eyes have gone all soft and intense, I know that she means exactly what I think she means.

On the way to my bedroom, we pass the golden retrievers. They're lying by the closed door to the yoga room, and when I reach down to pet them, they bare their teeth.

Kara asks what's wrong with them, and I tell her they're just playing, that it was a friendly growl.

We head on into my bedroom and get it on. It's quite fun, because I care about Kara, and I feel strongly that she cares about me.

I even light two candles on my dresser and turn off the lights. It's highly romantic.

Things are going very well. I'm making love to her more passionately than I've ever made love to anyone. Certainly more than the twins from New York. I have to say, we're both enjoying ourselves immensely, and every now and then, I'll look over through the window and see lovely LA at three in the morning, and then look down at lovely Kara. Everything's just beautiful tonight, and I'm starting to think that maybe things will be all right, when I hear a noise.

I'm sure Kara can't hear it, because she's making some noise of her own, but it chills my blood. It's the sound of a door opening very slowly. Creaking. I hear the tags on the dogs' collars clinking, I hear them licking something, and then, through the open doorway of my bedroom, I see a hand, an arm, and then a head. Something drags itself out of the yoga room, slowly, impossibly across the floor.

I hate to do this to Kara, because she's awfully close, but I whisper, breathlessly, "The dogs are getting into something. Can you hold on a second?"

"Jim, what are you—"

"Be right back."

I hop down from the bed and run naked into the hall, closing the bedroom door behind me.

"Bad dogs!" I yell.

They growl, but I raise my hand to them, and they bolt off down the hallway into another part of the house.

I drag it back into the yoga room. I don't even know what this thing is. As I make it stop moving, I keep thinking that I'm stuck in this awful nightmare. I don't ever want to see it again.

When I finish, I wash up and walk back into my bedroom and climb into bed with Kara. She's lying naked on top of the covers, head propped up on one elbow.

"Sorry about that," I say, pressing my body up against hers. I can't tell if she's mad. I think she might be, but she kisses me anyway and pulls me back on top of her.

In the morning, Kara wakes up frantic, because she has an eleven o'clock recitation to teach. I tell her if she can drive a stick, that she's welcome to take the Defender.

I walk her out, and we spend a minute saying all that stuff men and women are supposed to say to each other after a night like we had.

When she's gone, I walk around the side of the house to a tool shed. Inside, I find a shovel and set about digging a hole a hundred feet or so down the hillside from my patio. It takes a long time, because the ground is very hard and dry. In the end, it's not too deep, but it'll have to do.

What's even harder than the digging is the dragging of that thing out of the yoga room, all the way across my patio, down the hill, and into the bushes.

The hole is in a particularly nice spot, shaded from the sun, surrounded by sagebrush. You'd have to really be looking for it to find it, so I feel pretty good about the whole deal.

I roll it into the ground, but I don't start filling in the hole right away. I just stand there, staring down at it. It helps if I imagine that this thing I'm burying is all of the shit that's inside of me. I'm a firm believer that if you want to reach self-actualization or enlightenment, or whatever that really good place is called, you have to kill a part of yourself.

It's kind of like that scene in *The Empire Strikes Back* when Luke Skywalker is visiting the little green guy, and he goes down in that hole in the ground and fights the guy in the black cape. Well, after Luke kills him with his light sword, he looks down into the black mask and sees his own face. It's like he had to kill a part of himself to become a better human being.

That's similar to what I'm doing here. It's very metaphorical.

Chapter 25

phones Brad ~ swigs vodka ~ mulls over his amnesia and the impending automobile accident ~ into the ravine

I almost forget to call Brad. It's not that he's an essential component of what I'm getting ready to do, but it may expedite my rescue if someone misses me.

So I call him up, and he doesn't even say hello or anything.

Just answers, "Where in the hell have you been?"

"I had a late night."

"Another late night?"

"Yeah."

"I've been calling you all morning, and it's two o'clock now. You still want to get some work done today?"

"That's why I'm calling you."

"Are you fucked up?"

"No, of course—"

"'Cause don't even come to my house if you are. I'm not in the mood to fuck around. We have real work to do. I talked to Tom yesterday, and he's ready to see it. Like next week."

"All right. I'm on my way. See you in five."

Brad hangs up.

On my way out, I stop by the bar and open another bottle of vodka. I take four big swallows and head for the door, eyes watering.

The vodka kicks as I tear down Laurel Canyon. I'm feeling so happy about everything, and it's not just the alcohol. I told you about how I'd been forgetting things lately. For instance, a few minutes earlier, when Brad mentioned that "Tom was ready to see it," I had no idea what he was talking about. I don't know Tom from Adam. And apparently, Brad and I are writing a screenplay, but I couldn't tell you what it was about. And at Rich's party last night, I didn't know anyone who seemed to know me. Even my childhood has become a fog. For instance, I know for a fact that I grew up in the mountains near Missoula, Montana, but I have these inexplicable memories of a small town in North Carolina.

Perhaps the most frightening aspect of my amnesia, is that I'm beginning to doubt my acting ability. I'm an Oscar winner. I have the statue to prove it. But if I'm forgetting things as rudimentary as where I was born and who my friends are, how can I be sure my acting hasn't lapsed? And I'm supposed to read for the lead role in the new Harvey Wallison picture next week? You don't walk into that situation *wondering* if you can act.

The top's down on my Porsche, and the warm Pacific sun rains down through the trees.

I smell the forest all around me.

The ravine is just ahead, but instead of sailing on over, I bring my Porsche to a stop in the middle of the road, take a deep breath, and buckle my seatbelt.

My heart pounds.

It's a steep descent into that ravine. I hear a car climbing the hill below, and it occurs to me that I should do it now.

Close my eyes.

Punch the gas.

When they find me, I'll be bruised but intact.

Maybe a broken bone or two, a few cuts, a bump on the head.

I'll lay down there until someone finds me. I hope it doesn't take long. At least Brad is expecting me. That was exceptionally clever on my part.

The doctors will scan and probe and test and scan again, but they won't find anything to explain my amnesia. They'll be perplexed as to why I don't remember a thing about this life, or any other.

But my condition will be accepted. I was in a car wreck. No one will question that. And everyone will fall all over themselves to teach me about my beautiful life.

The other car is close. Another ten seconds, and it will be too late.

I jam my foot into the gas and accelerate toward the edge.

Then I'm falling, flipping, trees and shrubs and sky rushing by, the windshield cracked, a life passing before my eyes that is not mine.

MONTANA

Chapter 26

the thawing lake ~ tea with Pam ~ reads his paper ~ debates whether to ask Pam about who he was ~ Montana sky

My nose itches, and the lake is still half-frozen. I heard the ice splintering again last night. The remnants of this past winter—the iced lake, the snowpack on the mountains—seem artificial on a morning like this, when the trees are budding and a sweater is sufficient to keep a body warm.

I hear Pam walking back through the grass. She sets a tray on the folding table beside me.

"My nose itches," I say.

She rubs her index finger under my nose.

"Thank you."

"I made tea for us."

She fills our teacups.

The sun just reaches over that fin-like mountain at the other end of the lake.

"Did you bring my sunglasses?" I ask her.

"Sure did."

She sets my cup of tea in front of me and puts on my shades.

I drink tea, even hot tea, through a long, skinny straw.

Pam sits down beside me in the grass with her cup.

They tell me she's only my nurse, but she feels more like a sister. She doesn't sport nurse clothing. She wears jeans and a wool sweater. She's attractive.

"That man called again this morning," she tells me, and I ask which man she's referring to. I still have to be reminded of things a lot. That may never change.

"The man who called yesterday, and the day before, and the day before that."

"What does he want?"

"To see you."

"What did you say his name was?"

"Bo Dunkquist." From the way she says his name, I can tell that she's had to answer that question several times.

I don't know if I know him. I don't know much of anything really. For instance, right now there's a piece of paper in my pocket that tells me who I am and how I came to be this way, but I couldn't tell you what's written on that paper. And when I say "this way," I mean paralyzed from the neck down and scarred from third-degree burns over seventy percent of my body. That I do remember. The scarring part especially. Sometimes, I forget that I can't move, but I never forget what my face looks like, all smooth and hairless. I'm glad I don't forget, because it'd be an awful thing to have to see for the first time, day after day after day.

But don't feel sorry for me please. I'm not in any pain now, and I have no memories of when I was.

"I want to read my paper," I say. This woman, whose name I've forgotten, reaches into my pocket, pulls it out, and unfolds it for me. It's sort of funny—I remember that I have this paper, but I never remember what it says. You'd think if I could remember the one thing, I could remember the other.

I read it. I think I read it at least once a day, but I'm not sure:

Your name is James Jansen. You are 43 years old. Right now you are at your cabin in the mountains of Montana near the town of Woodworth. You are paralyzed from the neck down. Your nurse's name is Pam. She lives with you and will help you with anything you need. Your sister lives nearby in Missoula. Her name is Courtney, and she's 37. You were injured four years ago in an automobile accident when you lost control of your car and crashed into a ravine. You were in a coma in St. Anthony Medical Center in Los Angeles, California, until last September.

Before the accident, you were a very famous actor. You won the Oscar (a very prestigious award) in 20—, for your role in Down From the Sleeping Trees. You're holding it right now. Pam will tell you more about your acting career if you would like to know.

Today is April 15, 20—

I look down into my lap. There is in fact a shiny gold statue between my legs, gleaming in the sun.

Wind comes across the water and blows the paper out of my lap into the bright grass beside Pam. I hear the wind moving through the fir trees. Chimes jingle on the back porch of the cabin.

I start to ask Pam about who I was before the car wreck, but I stop. I'll bet I ask her that every day, and I'll bet she gets sick of having to tell me. Or maybe I just think I ask her every day, and so I never do. Perhaps I've had this same train of thought thirty days in a row.

So I don't say anything. It's easier to sit here and not think and stare at the lake and the mountains and the evergreens.

I'm not sad.

Not at all.

I don't feel much of anything except contentment to be out in this glorious morning.

Even if she were to tell me things about my old self, I don't think it would move me any more than the memory of a dream, because the only thing real to me is this moment—the wind-stirred lake and Pam and the blue Montana sky.

About the Author

BLAKE CROUCH is the author of DESERT PLACES, LOCKED DOORS, and ABANDON, which was an IndieBound Notable Selection last summer, all published by St. Martin's Press. His newest thriller, SNOWBOUND, also from St. Martin's, was released in 2010. His short fiction has appeared in Ellery Queen's Mystery Magazine, Alfred Hitchcock's Mystery Magazine, THRILLER 2, and other anthologies, including the new SHIVERS VI anthology from Cemetery Dance. In 2009, he co-wrote "Serial" with J.A. Konrath, which has been downloaded over 350,000 times and topped the Kindle bestseller list for 4 weeks. That story and ABANDON have also been optioned for film. Blake lives in Durango, Colorado. His website is www.blakecrouch.com.

Blake Crouch's Works

Andrew Z. Thomas thrillers
Desert Places
Locked Doors
Break You

Other works
Draculas with J.A. Konrath, Jeff Strand and F. Paul Wilson
Abandon
Snowbound
Famous
Run
Perfect Little Town (horror novella)
Serial with Jack Kilborn
Serial Uncut with J.A. Konrath and Jack Kilborn
Bad Girl (short story)
Killers (with Jack Kilborn)
Shining Rock (short story)
*69 (short story)
On the Good, Red Road (short story)
Unconditional (short story)
Remaking (short story)
The Meteorologist (short story)
The Pain of Others (novella)
Four Live Rounds (collected stories)
Six in the Cylinder (collected stories)
Fully Loaded (complete collected stories)

Coming soon…
Killers Uncut (with J.A. Konrath)
Serial Killers Uncut (with J.A. Konrath)
Stirred (with J.A. Konrath)

Visit Blake at www.BlakeCrouch.com

Printed in Great Britain
by Amazon